Plum's Grand Tour

NOVELS
Hackles Rise and Fall
Quentin and the Bogomils

HISTORY
Publishing and Bookselling
  Part I by Frank Mumby
  Part II 1870–1970 by Ian Norrie

LOCAL HISTORY/TOPOGRAPHY
The Book of Hampstead (*ed., with Mavis Norrie*)
The Book of the City (*ed.*)
Heathside Book of Hampstead and Highgate (*ed.*)
The Book of Westminster (*ed.*)
Hampstead, Highgate Village and Kenwood

Plum's Grand Tour

a farce

by
Ian Norrie

Macdonald and Jane's · London

© Ian Norrie 1978

ISBN 0 354 04325 0

Published by Macdonald and Jane's Publishers Ltd.
Paulton House
8 Shepherdess Walk
London N1

Made and printed in Great Britain by
Richard Clay (The Chaucer Press) Ltd, Bungay, Suffolk

For Amanda and Jessica
who could have been Simon and Brian.

Part One

The caravan swayed wildly in front of them. Bernard nosed out but Penny cried, 'No!' sharply, as she saw a huge truck bearing down upon them through the avenue of plane trees.

'Then there are two cars, and a brow of hill.'

From the back seat Donald pronounced, 'I would have all caravans off the road, dear heart, as I've said before. They're a social menace. Even a dangerous one. I would cancel their licences.'

'That's a bit pas de tolerant,' said Bernard, nosing out again, then quickly withdrawing in the face of flashing headlights. 'Some people couldn't afford to come to bloody abroad if they had to stay in hotels. Live and let live.'

'Live and let die,' was Donald's sanguine comment. 'But you are right, dear heart, not to take risks.' He sighed, fretfully, attempting to relax, folding his arms on his ample paunch.

'The children . . .' murmured Bernard, as though it might be acceptable for adults to sacrifice themselves on the roads of France, and then, noticing in his driving mirror his twin sons rampaging over the luggage in the open boot of the estate car, shouted, 'Get back on your seats, you boys, at once. Maintenant! I can't see what's coming up behind. Do as I say or we go back to Dover.'

'It was nice there,' said Brian, aged ten-and-a-half, but two hours younger than his brother. 'Had a smashing castle.'

'I'd rather go back to Calais,' said Simon. 'Smashing sands, *there*.'

'There'll be sands enough where you're going,' said Bernard, which was not strictly true because they were headed for what Henry James would have called mid-most France, unmitigated France, far from sea or beach.

'We'll play counting Renaults,' Penny suggested, appeasingly.

1

'We've done that.'

'Then count the British cars.'

'They've run out.'

'You really,' Donald announced, 'only see British cars when you stay on the N-roads. Les Routes Nationales. We are always so far off the beaten track that, personally, I shall be more than customarily amazed if we encounter anything less homespun than a hay wagon for the next one hundred killoms.'

'You *are* supposed to be guiding us, Donald,' Penny reminded him.

'And in any case,' added the driver, 'the caravan in front has a very large G.B. on its backside.'

'I do wish you'd get past it, dear heart.'

Bernard, falling in with this sentiment, chanced a leftwards movement, and Penny advised, 'I think so' from her hazardous front-seat-passenger position. Bernard honked loud and long, accelerated to 70 to pass the caravan (whose driver went up to 75) and halfway through his manoeuvre, was greeted by an oncoming car flashing frantically. 'Christ,' gasped Penny, but Bernard, revving to the very floor, murmured soothingly, 'Beaucoup de temps' and, in an agony of hoots and glaring headlamps, moved over just in time, in front of the caravan, the driver of which added his own illuminations to the occasion. They were projected on to a steep camber from which they swerved back into the middle of the road facing an open tunnel of trees for the next three kilometres. 'Alors!' proclaimed Bernard, recovering his composure. 'Or rather a-*lors*! Marvellous these French roads. Très, I always say, merveilleux. These wonderful avenues des arbres. Really does take the old chaude out of driving in warm weather.' He pulled at his dashing little beard, grown some years before despite Penny's disapproval.

No one commented until Donald, who was privately much unnerved, turned to his map and remarked, 'There ought to be a turning to the right about here, to take us down to St Martin-sur-Cadeau. It's a white road on the map. Probably not on yours at all, Penny.'

'I think,' Bernard commented, 'I saw the sign as we overtook the caravan. So we've missed it.'

'I'm surprised you saw anything as you overtook the caravan.' Donald lit a cigarette and hoped the boys did not notice that he was trembling.

'There'll be another turning.'

'You can't always guarantee it in France, Bernard. We're not at home now.'

'Don't I realize it, Moose-year.'

'At least you might make an effort to get that right, dear heart.' Donald made phonetic sounds of impeccable correctness.

'Well, dekko votre carte, Monsoo. For the next right-hand turn.'

'I'm trying to but you're going so fast.'

'It's the road. I have to. And it is passage protégé. Our right of way. I have to drive in the middle of the road. It's the camber.'

'They don't like it.'

'Which is why they do it all the time. Anyhow, there's nothing coming.'

A vivid flashing of lights occurred behind him causing Bernard to hurl his vehicle swiftly vergewards to allow a seething limousine to overtake him at 110 m.p.h.

'Fucking lunatic!'

'Fucking lunatic,' chorused Brian and Simon.

'Where's this turning then?' Bernard slowed down to

3

about 68. 'I'm not the sort of driver to ignore advice from the navigator. You know that. I don't just belt on and on.' (The speedometer registered 80.) 'Just tell me! Is there a way round?' He looked before him and rejoiced. 'For crying out bleeding alors, what a road!' He put his foot down.

'What does "alors" mean?' asked Simon.

'It's an expression, lovey.'

'But what's it *mean*, Mum?'

'You tell him, Bernard.'

'It means . . . "Now then!" . . . It means "Right!" . . . "So there we are." It means "Whereas" or "Therefore"; even, "Even so!". It means lots of things. Very expressive word. Can't do without it in Frogland. Alors! What a road!'

Brian asked, 'So what does "bleeding alors" mean?'

At this moment Bernard touched the 100 and roared at Donald, 'Let me know when you think there'll be a turning.' The older man relaxed his hold on the flimsy Michelin map in his grasp, and it was blown out through the sunshine roof and into the sprawling countryside. The twins were delirious. 'You can't go much faster,' shrieked Brian, ecstatically, 'according to your speedometer.'

'Whaa-at?' roared Bernard and then, mercifully, saw a road sign far ahead. 'Can't see what it says.' He braked. 'I'm sure we ought to go right here. Can anyone read it?' He braked harder and there was a smell of scorching rubber.

'Yes,' said Penny. '*Priorité à droite.*'

They stopped miraculously, just short of calamity, as a three-piece articulated truck with trailers swept by. Donald said, with assumed nonchalance, reading the signpost as he felt for his hip flask, '*St Martin-sur-Cadeau*, 8 Killoms. A, as you might say, dear heart, à droite.'

Near St Martin they spent the night, but the G.B. caravan arrived ahead of them.

4

The adventure had begun two months before in the offices of the *Sunday Wanderer*, the colour supplement of the *Sunday Sabbatical*, Lord Proggle's weekly publication angled to encourage the affluent to spend ever more wildly and exotically to the benefit of cruise organizers, travel agents and other entrepreneurs advertising in his not widely, but very selectively, read journal. Bernard Plum, a forty-year-old non-graduate who had failed to fulfil the promise shown in his primary school days, was employed as a feature writer on the *Wanderer* on the strength of having published, many years earlier, an account of a bicycle ride over the Alps, a book which had been a minor bestseller in its day, and even remained in print in a large type edition designed for those who had ceased travelling long since as late as 1974, when the events related here took place. Bernard's immediate superior, an associate editor of the *Wanderer*, was Monty d'Etaing who, having once walked all the way from Gibraltar to the tip of Lapland, for the most part in a howling gale, felt himself, at fifty, one up on his entire staff.

Monty remarked one day over the office intercom to Bernard, 'Our readers have to be tested. Can you spare a moment? It's something which should appeal to you.'

Bernard, who was hearing, in as far as he could be said to be listening, for the thirty-third time, another colleague's plod by plod description of a re-enactment of Stevenson's donkey ride through the Cevennes, gladly vacated his desk.

'I flatly refuse to go to the Moon,' he insisted as he strode into d'Etaing's office, patting the rubber tyres which were already a talking point between him and the manager of his local menswear shop who was finding it increasingly difficult to sell him garments off the peg.

'Much nearer home, dear fellow,' replied Monty. 'My father's ain country, in fact, as my mother would say.'

5

Monty was inordinately proud of his Franco-Scottish heritage and hinted at links with that Mary whom the great Elizabeth reluctantly condemned to death. 'Listen,' he said, 'we want a series on remote places in France – on the sort of hotels which have red rocking-chair symbols in *Michelin*. The kind which, when anyone says, "Where did you spend your holiday, old thing?" you reply, frightfully bored, of course, "We went, actually, to Flangoux". And they say, "Where exactly is that, I forget?" trying not to appear too ignorant. So you say, off-handedly, "Not *all* that far from Randillac, you most know it." Then they look frankly puzzled, so you add, "No? I'll tell you then. It's a turning off . . ."'

'I take it that the accompanying piped-music has come on by now?'

Monty gave a sour look and continued . . . '"*A turning off* the road from Luzy-les-Trois-Eglises, not far from the junction of the Main Tours—Angoulême highway. Now supposing you were coming from Chenonceaux . . ."'

'Yes, yes, I take your point, but why?'

'That's where they have to use their powers of deduction.'

'As well as their maps?'

'As well as their maps. But another thing. You mustn't actually select too many red rocking-chair hotels from *Michelin*. Although you will have to rely on that source a great deal. But if you overdo it you may make it too simple.' He wriggled his wrists in expert parody of a Frenchman expressing 'comme-ci, comme-ça.'

'I see.' Bernard twitched at his beard, which was always comforting to him; that was why he had grown it. 'I'm selecting the hotels?'

'Right. You can stay away for three months, and I want you to fit in at least three places a week, once you've got going, so that we can run a series from immediately before Christmas until late summer.'

'Three months on the old continong has a certain appeal . . . but to stay in France *all* the time . . . Italy . . .?'

'France only. If it's successful you may get to do Italy next year.'

'I take it I'm allowed to tell the readers all about the hotels but must conceal the actual names . . .?'

'*And* the names of the towns the hotels are in. Even the departements. You will give them clues. Make it as difficult as possible, mind you, because the prizes are very expensive to us.'

'Like what?'

'Like sending the winners on a fourteen-day tour of the fourteen most desirable places of their choice, at our expense. That's one reason for restricting it to France for the time being. France is nearer. Another thing . . .' Monty became very serious, all signs of humour vanished from his face. 'The Lord is very keen on this story himself. He seems to wish to impress some of his intellectual friends. Already he's talking about the series as *his* idea. So watch it.'

'When do I start?'

'As soon after Easter as possible. Then you can be through before la saison saison commences. You don't want to be over there once the natives and the tourists are choking up the hotels.'

'How considerate. But it does mean that as soon as I return I shall be wanting to go away on holiday with the family . . .'

Monty shrugged his shoulders. 'We all have our problems . . . You're a lucky man. If I had your chance . . .'

Yes, thought Bernard, and if Lord Proggle weren't so interested in it, you would certainly have taken it. Well, that's your privilege.

As he drove home, he wondered how to get out of the assignment which, he could see, spelt trouble. Apart from anything else, his French was so inadequate, for all that he liked to pretend to Penny and the boys that he was something of a linguist. Not that Penny was taken in.

He arrived at his North London home very unenthusiastic about the project but Penny soon attended to that. She beamed with pleasure as she cooked a moussaka. 'What a splendid opportunity. It'll be a wonderful experience for the boys.'

'This is not a family jaunt, darling. The boys aren't in on it. That's what worries me. Having to be away for three months.'

'Don't be silly, Bernie. We shall come too.'

'What about their schooling?'

'So, you're going to start worrying about that, now?'

'Must be responsible, old dear.' He grinned and Penny sat down, folded her arms. When she smiled, it was with her eyes and Bernard could not resist her. 'It is against the law,' he complained, mildly, 'to take them out of school. You're always telling me.'

'We can get over that. It'll be an educational trip. In any case the authorities are notoriously lax about enquiring into absences. They should be more rigid but, mercifully, they're not. It'll suit us. Don't you want us to come?'

'You know I do . . .'

'Right then.'

And he did want Penny to come, couldn't bear the thought of separation. Only he didn't actually relish going himself. 'How can I possibly afford to take the three of you away for all that time?'

'If you can't fiddle it on expenses, I'll make use of

8

Mummy's money.'

That clinched it. Penny's mother had willed her estate with the not very strictly enforceable instructions that a substantial part should be used to initiate her grandchildren into the rigours of foreign travel.

Bernard walked about the large, bay-windowed living-room overlooking the Osidge valley. 'It would be lovely but there is the problem of language.'

'I'll learn it. Take a crash course.'

'Not time. Job starts immediately after Easter. You wouldn't make it.'

Penny, a realist, and no linguist, said, pulling a poker face, 'We'll have to take Donald then.'

Bernard shuddered. Donald Ardrake was his bachelor uncle, a retired antiquarian bookseller who had made his fortune easily and early in life by detecting several items of incunabula, on which he was an expert, in the attic of a Midlands' mansion. They belonged to an elderly lady, the last of her line, who fell in love with him and, conveniently, died leaving him all her possessions, apart from the house and grounds which went to the nation.

Since World War Two, when he had been in intelligence because of his knowledge of France and the French, Donald had not worked for his living, so far as Penny and Bernard knew. They understood him to be rich and, therefore, able to pay his way whilst ministering to their language difficulties in the sixth republic. 'What better,' exclaimed Penny, 'than Donald for this little job?'

'Can we stand him for three months?'

'We must. No one else could afford to come. Open a bottle.'

Penny saw an unexpectedly pleasant release from suburban life for many weeks to come; Bernard reached out a practised hand for the drawer where the corkscrew lay, and had serious qualms about the venture.

Sunday morning in Ikin Copse, Hertfordshire. At 23, The Spinney, an open-plan, two-and-a-half storey 1970s structure in brick and wood, Adrian Longhorn, lecturer in Modern French History at the University of Ware, and Tina, his wife, lay in bed with the Sunday papers untidily spread around them. The bed, and that comprised ninety per cent of the bedroom itself, was set on a giant shelf rising above and covering half of the first floor living-room, so that it formed a balcony reached by a long, straight staircase up the wall of the chamber. Adrian adored it. It made him feel regal to lie in bed high above the living quarters. Tina felt exposed as though she were on a film set with hundreds of technicians ogling her. Even when they made love which, it being Sunday morning, they recently had, she had the uneasy impression of being watched. She pulled a supplement of the *Observer* towards her, saying, 'What is it we have to feel deprived about this week? Oh, dawling, I simply cannot live without a two-sink kitchen. Shirley Conran says so.'

Adrian yawned over the *Times* colour supplement. 'They're setting out to ruin Andorra next week. "The first of three articles by experts on the tiny Pyrenean nation perched between France and Spain in wildly impressive terrain." I can just about accept the idea of one expert on Andorra, but three! That's ridiculous.'

'God, they're boring, these papers,' said Tina, as she said

every Sunday morning. 'Why don't we give up some of them?'

'The *Sabbatical* can go as far as I'm concerned. It's getting far too trendy.'

'They do send you books to review.'

'Yes. I suppose I'd better go on with it.' He began idly to tear up a business supplement and to make paper darts which he aimed at the elaborate mobile serving as a chandelier. (There weren't, of course, bulbs in it because how could they conveniently have been changed? The lighting was concealed, so much so that reading after dusk was a strain.)

'Hold on,' said Tina. 'The *Wanderer* is coming up with something in your line. "Another new series planned for the autumn can win you a fortnight in some of the most secluded and tranquil of French hotels. Details of this exciting new series will be announced shortly."'

'But we know *all* the secluded and tranquil hotels in France.'

'Therein lies the subtlety of the modern Sunday Heavy. They get at you psychologically by making you feel superior to them. By the way those property people are getting at us again. I think we're about the only ones who won't sell.' She leapt quickly from bed, gathered up several sheets of newsprint into a ball and flung it over the balcony. It was the same every Sunday morning in the Longhorn home. Supplement after supplement went over the balcony, then they had it off again before descending to grind coffee and play songs of the Auvergne on the hi fi. The Longhorns did not, as may be imagined, attend church but they could scarcely have behaved with stricter ritual if they had.

St Martin-sur-Cadeau boasted a church with a roof so low-slung at some points that irreverent burghers had been known to lean against it for support whilst en route from one bar to the next. It dominated a side of the main *place* which, roughly hexagonal in shape, came to jabbering life on market days, when the prodigiously spacious Café du Commerce, covering quite half an acre with its various public rooms, served pernod, wine and cider (but especially pernod) to the loquacious stallholders, and to the residents who searched for bargains among the gaily-coloured awnings. In the *place* were also a branch of the Banque Agricole, two rows of shabby houses and a score of shops. The foundations of these buildings had been laid centuries before but their visible structures had been so altered and savaged by fire, warfare and modernization, that the most perceptive of architectural commentators would have been hard-pressed to date the whole or the parts. There was but one overall impression. Poverty.

The brickwork needed repointing, the window frames repainting, the roofs retiling. The gutters had gaping holes in them, the chimneys lurched drunkenly. But this was all outward show, nothing more than a hopeful tax dodge, a reaffirmation of faith in one's duty to avoid the demands of the inland revenue whilst keeping one's fortune unimpaired under the rotting floorboards.

The pavements of St Martin, where they existed at all, were unswept. In the gathering grit of the Jardin Publique men and boys played boule. It had all been thus for centuries, apart from the motor cars and the electric lighting. Donald viewed it with affection and noticed a sign, mostly hidden by a sprawling chestnut tree, on which he could just discern the words La Vielle Ferme de Brieu. 'If we wish to claim our beds before they are let to some frightful

Proustian searching for fresh evidence to sift, we ought to take that turning over there and get on our way. You know how early they stop serving dinner in the country. And that's disastrous for my ulcers.'

They all knew Donald didn't have ulcers but the pretence was part of the price they paid for his company, and belief in them assured Donald of frequent stops for food and drink.

Penny asked, 'Are you sure you can get through there?'

'Perhaps it's passage protégé.'

'Shut up, Simon.'

'I do know how to steer.' Bernard scraped the bumper lightly against a flaking edge of wall. 'There's no need to ask which way?' Before him was a narrow track between dishevelled buildings, just wide enough for his vehicle. As he rounded the next bend (without further damage) he saw, in front of him, a bridge.

Further investigation proved it to be a hastily slung pontoon, left over from a rapid Allied advance some thirty years before. The units were tenuously connected and there were altogether too many gaps to make for comfortable motoring.

'There must be another way round. Got your map, Donald?'

'It blew out of the car.'

'That's a fine thing.'

'Is it my fault if your car doesn't have a roof?'

'Well, bloody hell . . .' Bernard tugged at his beard. 'There must be an autre chemin, comme ils dits. Let's bloody voir for it. You go that way, Donald. I'll go this.'

Ten minutes later the two men were reunited and Bernard was not altogether pleased when his uncle reported that not only had he sighted a more substantial bridge along *his* way, but that he had watched the G.B. car and caravan crossing it.

13

'Return to the square, dear heart. Then turn right. Right again. Should be impossible to miss it, as they say.'

'Comme ils bloody dits.' Bernard leapt into the driving seat.

'Wouldn't you prefer, dear heart, to take the boys with you?'

Penny jumped from the car, blushing. 'Brian! Simon! We're going.'

'Brian's going down now, aren't you Brian?' Simon, all but immersed in the waters of the Cadeau, imitated one of his father's ancient radio voices.

'Come out of the river at once.'

'Glug, glug,' gurgled Simon, ghoulishly. 'A circle marks the spot where Brian Plum went down for the last time. Don't forget the diver, sir!'

Brian spoilt the effect by rushing naked from behind a bush.

'Simon, come out, at once.'

'I'm coming up now, sir.'

'You don't know what you're talking about and, anyway, he didn't say it like that.'

'I'm just imitating you, Dad.' Simon jumped on to the bank and sprayed his father with filthy water, as he shook himself with the abandon of a wet puppy.

'I don't know, dear heart, that I should actually turn in here . . .' Bernard was nosing the car between gateposts leading on to an expansive ploughed meadow, where tips of cereal could already be observed.

'But where else?' They had followed an increasingly rutted

track for over a mile. 'I can hardly go straight on.' Bernard indicated a brambled footpath heavily overgrown with cow parsley.

Penny commented, 'Perhaps we've taken a wrong turning?'

'Any other bright suggestions?'

'Yes, let's go back to Calais.'

'Shut up, Simon.'

'The I.G.N. quite clearly . . .'

'The what, Donald? Please try not to talk obscurely. It's been a long day.'

'I have, since losing my Michelin map, got out of the pocket the local large-scale map drawn by the Institut Géographique Nationale. The – I should say "la" – La Vielle Ferme de Brieu is clearly marked on it.'

'And where is it in relation to this particular spot of verdure?'

'Bernie . . .'

'Sorry Pen. Tiring day.' Bernard remembered his promise not to be rude to Donald.

'Where indeed? I suggest you don't go through this field of burgeoning maize in your wily, wizened way, but turn back until we reach that junction where the wrecked tractor lay in the ditch.'

'That's a good mile back.'

'I just make the suggestion.'

'Why didn't you get this bleeding I.B.M. map out before?'

'Because I couldn't, dear heart, bleeding find it. And it's I.G.N. Institut Géo . . .'

'Yes, yes, yes.' He mustn't be rude to Donald, but he'd made no promise about the car. He reversed aggressively. He punched his gear lever in and out, brushed numerous items of vegetation, hurled the vehicle this way and that and, eventually, retraced his way along the pitted lane at a speed which showed little consideration for the springs and none at all for the passengers.

At last the ditched tractor was sighted.

'Now where, please?'

'Left, I venture to suggest. Straight on would take us back to St Martin. And,' Donald added as Bernard turned out of one wagon way and into another, 'there should shortly be a crossroads in the middle of a copse. With luck there'll be a signpost to the old farm. La Vielle Ferme,' he enunciated slowly to the boys, who regarded him with loathing.

There wasn't a signpost and, in the already well-leaved copse, it was growing dark so that Donald had difficulty reading his map.

'It must be straight on.'

'Must it.' Bernard drove straight on muttering, 'Tout droit, tout droit. You'd think that would mean all to the right, but it means straight on. Very droll tongue this French.'

'I think it's better once you've learnt it, Dad.'

'Thank you, Brian.'

Quite quickly they reached a made-up road with a sign one way to St Martin-sur-Cadeau (2 km) and the other to La Vielle Ferme (1 km).

'In my wily, wizened way, I've almost got us there.'

'But there must have been a more direct route. Where did we go wrong?'

'No, darling, don't look at the map now. We're nearly there.'

'Probably won't be any rooms left . . .'

They arrived in the drive of an old farmhouse where a short-fuselaged alsatian sprinted out to deliver a venomous welcome.

'Don't stroke him,' warned Penny.

'Shall I close the roof?'

'Just blow your horn to let them know we're here.'

The alsatian was joined by three others of its kind who stood and barked frenziedly as the car stopped in front of the ivy-covered building. No one appeared to greet them but in a field beyond the farm they could see the G.B. caravan and people moving about. As the dogs continued their frantic yowling the Plums and Donald sat bemused. At last an elderly woman in a baggy black dress, with an apron tied round her waist, ran round the side of the building and scolded the dogs, who withdrew several yards but still looked hungrily on their prey.

'Voulez-vous decendre, m'sieur?'

'Non,' replied Donald, cautiously, and stood up in the back seat, the top part of his body craned inelegantly forward to clear the partially opened roof of the car. ('Don't forget to call her cher coeur,' advised Bernard.) Donald asked for accommodation for the night, two doubles and one single, and threw the woman into hysterics. She delivered a long, incomprehensible oration and then ran to the farmhouse door where she turned, shrieked a few more rapid sentences, and disappeared.

'What did she say?'

'I think, Penny, she has gone to ask the patron. It'll be all right.' Donald adopted a soothing, experienced-traveller tone. 'They always carry on like this. Let us go in.'

'What about the wolves?'

'They won't touch us now.' Donald got out first and the others reluctantly stepped on to the drive. 'Not unless they taste blood.' Nevertheless, even he was pleased to make the sanctuary of the farmhouse where the woman who had harangued them was poring over a register of rooms with a neatly dressed young man who was gesturing with a ballpoint pen.

After much questioning of the aproned-woman, and heavy frowns at the would-be residents, interspersed with obsequious smiles and mutters of 'à votre service, monsieur', several keys were removed from a rack, and the woman commanded the visitors to follow her. She proceeded up flights of winding staircase and along numerous dark corridors, with hidden steps and other hazards, and showed them, beyond creaking barn-type doors, rooms with two beds, rooms with three beds, rooms so crammed with beds that it was some wonder that they could also accommodate wardrobes, dressing-tables and chairs. There were, it transpired, at least twelve rooms immediately vacant so they selected three in one wing near the top of a staircase.

'Voulez-vous manger, m'sieur?'

'Oui, merci.'

'A quelle heure?'

'Sept et demi. Huite moins quinze. Peut-être. Alors.'

'Oui. Comme vous voulez, m'sieur.'

All was sweetness, all was light. The rooms were there. The dinner would be there. 'So why did there have to be all that fuss?' Penny sank, exhausted, on to a bed.

'It's the French way, dear heart. Shall we meet in the bar for aperitifs at, say, seven-thirty?'

'I must have something long before that.'

'I can get us a drink,' whispered Bernard, as his uncle left them.

'Well, I should like cinzano with lots of ice and soda, and get cokes for the boys.'

'Per-shit, for me,' said Brian, giggling.

'Brian!'

'What's wrong with that, Mum?' All wide-eyed innocence.

'It says it on the bottle. P-S-S-C-H-I-T-T. I had it at that place . . .'

'Pair-sheet is correct,' said Bernard. 'I shan't be long.'

'Pair-sheet,' said both boys in unison, happily.

On the murky ground floor Bernard looked hopefully for a bar. He entered a room with a door ajar and was instantly halted by a massive oval table around which it was impossible to proceed because several wooden chairs, with high backs, blocked the way, leaving no more than a hint of space between them and two enormous sideboards. On the far wall of the room was a comfortless chaise-longue draped with antimacassars and three splay-legged footstools ranged decorously before it.

The aproned-woman appeared.

'M'sieur?'

'Ah. And alors. Bonne soir, mademoiselle – er – madame. Ou est le bar?'

'Nous n'avons pas de bar, m'sieur.'

'God, it isn't temperance is it?'

'M'sieur?'

'Je désire buvez, s'il vous plait.'

'Oui, m'sieur. Qu'est ce que vous voulez?'

'You're not dry then?'

'M'sieur?'

'Vous avez un chinzarno . . .?'

'Shinzarno?'

'Oui, chinzarno. Aperitif. Savez-vous?'

'Non, m'sieur. Un instant.' The woman ran into the hall screaming for the patron's wife who duly emerged from dark recesses of the house smiling inscrutably and asking, in floods of rapid French, what the gentleman desired.

Bernard produced a scribbling pad and wrote on it, *cinzano rouge*.

19

'Ah, cinzano! Oui, m'sieur. Un cinzano.'

'Merci.' He felt exhausted. 'Et aussi, madame . . . une bee-air, très grande et frais. Mais, avec le sanzarno – excusez-moi, madame, je dit, "*chin*-zarno" – c'est Italienne, nes pas? Excusez-moi. Je suis désolé. Je suis étranger. Alors, madame, avec le *san*zarno, le glace, et le zodarr. Zo-*darr*!' he repeated, smiling encouragingly, and hoping to woo the patron's wife out of the state of petrification into which this spiel had driven her. He didn't succeed.

'Un moment,' she muttered. 'Mon fils.' And she hastily withdrew.

In rather more than a moment a stocky man, moustached and nearly bald, looking more like her father than her son, and bearing every sign of having been overworked for centuries, presented himself and gabbled, 'Le patron est à Rouen pour les affaires du Marché Commun. Je m'excuse,' none of which Bernard understood. Then, in English, he added, 'You would like drink?'

Relief shone from Bernard's eyes. An English-speaking wog. Quel luck. 'Yes, may I have a sanzarno rouge with ice and soda. Zo-*darr*,' he went on as the man's expression became blank. 'You know, like visky zo-darr?'

'No, m'sieur, no visky.'

'I don't want whisky. Visky.'

'Pardon, m'sieur, un moment.' The balding man disappeared as Simon hurled himself down the stairs, yelling, 'It's orange pair-sheet we'd like, not lemon.'

'Shut up, Simon.'

'That's all you ever say. But they do two sorts. And we'd like the orange, please.'

'You'll be lucky to get either.'

'I suppose they can't understand your French.'

The balding man returned with a surly youth who said,

insolently, 'I am barman. What you would like, m'sieur?'

'Where is bar?'

'No bar, m'sieur. I show you.' Which was illogical but encouraging.

In the dining-room was a healthily stocked shelf of bottles. Bernard indicated the Cinzano Rouge. He went on to order Pschitt but all he got through was the word 'orange'. The young man nodded compliance and seemed also to understand that a large measure of ale was required.

'En chambre,' said Bernard grandly, and walked upstairs with dignity and a parched palate, narrowly avoiding contact with a sixteenth-century beam.

Fifteen minutes later the aproned-woman came to his room with a tray groaning under a bottle of Cinzano, a bucket of ice, an ancient soda syphon heavily tarnished, a two-litre wine bottle of local beer, two oranges pressées, and several fruit-juice sized glasses.

'Ca va!' she observed brightly.

'Ca va,' replied Bernard, defeated.

At seven-thirty, having drunk numerous small glassfuls of frothy warm beer, Bernard, his thirst unquenched, descended to meet Donald whom he found seated at a table outside the farmhouse in the evening twilight. He was sipping white wine.

'There's no bar in this dump. That could be a clue for my readers.'

'Hardly, dear heart. It is so often the case. But it doesn't mean there's nothing to drink. Join me in a delectable glass of Sancerre. Someone in these backwoods knows about wine.'

'Probably the absent patron. I think one of them said he was in Rouen with a marché commune or something.'

'That means common market. Probably negotiating the sale of his apples. He has fields and fields of them. Now sit down. Have a glass of wine, I find that nothing calms the soul more effectively than deliciously chilled white wine sipped in the open on a warm evening. How fortunate we are to have it so warm, so early. I remember such an evening at Saumur . . . it must have been about 1948 . . .' Donald launched into a lengthy reminiscence to which Bernard paid little heed as he sank most of the carafe of wine.

Thumping sounds as Simon and Brian jumped down stairs five at a time heralded renewed demands for 'pair-sheet'. Penny, who had had enough, asked if they might eat at once; Donald, noting the empty carafe, agreed. 'I suspect we'll have some excellent Norman fare here. It will be difficult for you to disguise it, Bernard-O. Anyhow, you must give your unfortunate readers some clues.'

A savage barking broke out as the caravanners entered the salle à manger with the alsatian pack snapping at their ankles.

A well-built, bearded young man in denims smiled good-naturedly and extended a hand to Bernard, saying, 'We're the poor relations. Caravanners. But we thought we'd treat ourselves to a properly cooked meal on the first night out. I'm Dick Oxenford. This is my wife, Dilys.'

Bernard responded affably. 'I'm Tony Cupboard. My wife, Jill. Our friend, Sir Aubrey Notten.'

Oh dear, thought Penny, I forgot to tell the boys.

'I say, Anthony, said Donald, who had been looking forward to the use of his pseudonym, 'why don't we invite

22

the Oxenfords to join us? We'll all have a splendid first-night-abroad meal together. We crossed today, too. I think we passed you on the road.'

Penny shuddered at the memory and Dick said, 'That shooting brake of yours can certainly travel. Just as well.'

The staff rearranged the tables in considerable uproar under Donald's direction while Dilys, a slender brunette, also dressed in denim and glowing with uncomplicated good health, noticed the shyness of the boys and said, smiling appealingly at Simon, 'What's your name?'

Simon responded cagily with a faint grin and looked towards his mother for guidance, but she was fighting off an alsatian. Not having overmuch imagination at this fatigued moment in his young life, he replied, '*I'm* Brian'. Brian, swiftly catching on, added 'And *I'm* Simon.'

Which makes me old Mother Hubbard, thought Penny, as the aproned-woman wrenched the hound away, driving it into a corner where it remained snuffling and seething with discontent until attracted by some commotion in the yard, whereupon all the wolves vacated the dining-room in a further crescendo of soprano whines, knocking several tables askew as they left.

Donald decided to take command and, recognizing Dick as potential group leader, opened his offensive with an authoritative, 'I would suggest these good people probably know more about selecting a balanced menu than we do. In short, should we allow le patron to know what will be best for us; have the set meal?'

'There's no à la carte here, Sir Aubrey,' said Dick disarmingly. 'You get what's coming, and I'm sure it's good.'

'Don't like frogs' legs, Simon,' said Simon, looking intently at Brian who replied, 'And I don't like snails, Brian,' after which they collapsed in giggles.

Donald, still tingling with pleasure at being addressed as Sir Aubrey, said, 'I don't know, in my wily wizened way, what we shall be eating, but I would recommend a really fragrant Sancerre, if there is anything appropriate with which to eat it.'

'We always drink the vin du pays, Sir Aubrey. Which,' added Dick, 'means cider and/or calvados.'

Donald sought desperately for an apposite maxim of La Rochefoucauld's with which to cap the conversation but his recall system was faultily programmed at that moment. 'No need to call me "Sir",' he said, instead, with a simper.

During dinner Dick talked engagingly and knowledgeably about France. He addressed himself to each of them in turn, joked with the boys and was mildly deferential to Donald, asking the older man for his opinion of the terrine and, later, of the caneton youvennais, and allowing himself to be poured a glass or two of Sancerre. Bernard warmed to him and began to visualize a continuing liaison which would assist his mission.

'Do you always come to this sort of place, Jill? I may call you "Jill"?'

'Please do, Dick. Everyone does.' The boys beamed appreciatively at their clever, self-controlled mother. ('Hi, Bri!' said Brian; 'Hi, Si!' responded Simon.) 'Yes,' Penny went on, 'we like places that are away from the tourist zones, where the food is good and the ambience pleasant . . .'

'What's "ambience", Mum?'

'It means, Brian, the surroundings, the general

24

atmosphere, dear heart, from ambient, I take it, which means to revolve, to encircle, to encompass. It is one of those French words for which there is no exact English equivalent, which is why we use it although, as you are probably aware, English is a much richer language than French, with many more words, and many finer shades of meaning than it is possible to achieve in French, which is why they borrow so much from us. However, as I say, sometimes *we* are indebted to them. And that is why we use the word your mother employed. Ambience. A good word.'

'I only asked what it meant.'

'Exactly.' Donald turned genially to Dick. 'It is what one can do with a language that I find so interesting. Now take English. You can invent your own endings and people frequently do. The most famous and yet simple example is this, I think you will agree. "Now look here, my good woman," I say to some – who shall I say? – some stallholder in a market whom I suspect of swindling me. "Now look here my good woman . . ." And she replies, arms akimbo, don't you think? Yes, arms definitely akimbo. She replies, "And who are you a good-womanning of?" It's a marvellous idiomatic use of the tongue. Or she might reply, "Don't you good-woman me" which is even more gorgeous . . . And then take . . .' Donald went on and on until the wolf pack burst into the room again, sending chairs flying.

Bernard took advantage of Donald's temporary silence to observe that 'One of the least endearing habits of the French is their unwillingness to ban dogs from dining-rooms, even though they pretend they have.'

'Yes, you often find the dog's head with the oblique sign through it in the Michelin, but you're so right, the proprietors seldom pay any regard to it.' Dick said he'd made quite a study of the subject. 'I've compiled a list in fact of quiet French farmhouses and hotels which really do ban them.'

'Not *farmhouses* surely, pet?'

'That's an exaggeration. But I do know some, Dil, where the dogs are kept in the yard.'

'I'd be awfully interested,' began Bernard. 'You see our itinerary is uncertain, as at this moment in time, and we have nothing definitely plotted about where we are staying. Right?'

Donald said he thought they had.

'No, Awb, it's frightfully flex-eeble.'

'I'd rather you didn't call me "Awb".'

'Sorry, Sir Dear-Heart.'

Dick said he'd be delighted to give some tips. 'How long you over here for?'

'About three months.'

'Really? You on a sabbatical?'

'You could put it that way. Might even call it a wander.'

'Lucky you.'

'How long's your holiday?' Penny asked Dilys.

'Dick doesn't tell me, but we come and go a lot, don't we pet?' She opened her large brown eyes and looked at Penny very sincerely and fixedly, like a cat, which made the other woman uncomfortable, so that she said, sharply, 'Come along, Simon. Bed.'

Simon didn't move. 'Now don't play about!'

'Why should Brian get up first,' said Brian, and Penny caught on. 'They're so alike I sometimes call them by each other's name,' she said weakly.

'How strange,' remarked Dilys. 'They look quite different to me.'

Donald took breakfast in his room but Bernard and Penny thought it would be simpler to sit at a table. The dining-room was peaceful with late spring sunshine pouring in so Penny suggested opening a window.

'They won't like it.'

'Why not, Dad?'

'The French have a thing about fresh air, Brian . . .'

'I'm Simon.'

'When we're alone you're Brian.'

'I have to think of myself as Simon. That's why I'm twitching.'

'I *don't* twitch, Frogs Legs.' Simon punched his brother. 'You're bleeding alors, you are.'

'And you're pair-sheet.'

'. . . as I was saying the French will not tolerate fresh air, indoors, unless they want to hang blankets out of windows.'

Nevertheless, Penny went ahead and sniffed the air appreciatively. She returned to the table as the window slammed shut in a gust of wind.

'You didn't latch it.'

'There's nothing to latch it to. There isn't even a latch.'

'I cannot understand why they don't learn from us. It's just sheer insularity on their part.' Bernard propped the window open with a knife.

The aproned-woman came in bearing an enormous tray just as another gust of wind jerked the window partially to, with a violent whine.

'Pardon, m'sieur,' she said, setting down the tray on a nearby table, and firmly closed the window. 'Quel vent! La, la!'

Bernard was enraptured. She really had said, 'La, la!' France was living up to all his prejudices. Happily, he dunked a croissant into his coffee and Brian asked, 'Why isn't that rude here?'

'Dunking is an old Norman habit. Invented by the Conqueror.'

'Now you really are confusing them. Have some of this sumptuous butter and stop making such a mess.'

After breakfast they went into the wide gravelled forecourt and Bernard's good humour remained with him. 'Pas de chien,' he observed.

'What's Dad mean?'

'Not of dog,' explained Penny.

'You know perfectly well what I mean. Anyhow, they are pas. Perhaps someone has poisoned their water.'

Bernard turned his attention to the farmhouse and began to make architectural comments of the 'I-suppose-that-wing-was-added-after-the-revolution' variety. The boys were given permission to kick a ball. Dick hailed them from the caravan field and Donald descended, flourishing a paperback, announcing that he'd just found that most marvellous description of a dull Norman village in *Madame Bovary*, which no doubt they all recalled, but anyhow he would read it to them, which he did, in French, but none of them listened.

A noisy old Renault swept into view, circled the forecourt, blowing up clouds of dust, and came to a screeching halt beside Donald. A triple-chinned, double-paunched, middle-aged farmer stepped from the vehicle and shook everyone's hands enthusiastically. In passable English he hoped they'd had a comfortable night, that they would enjoy their stay on his farm, and apologized for not having been present on their arrival but he had been in Rouen on important Common Market business. He wagged his head to one side, winked prodigiously and said it was 'formidable'. He did not explain what was but instead informed them he had learned his English from the Allied soldiers who had been billeted at the farm during the war. Donald was instantly interested and told the farmer, whose name was Vesoul, that he had been in Intelligence. ('That's what he got his knighthood for,' Bernard explained to Dick.) An eager exchange of military experiences followed with Donald speaking always in French with a Parisian accent he had been perfecting for years, and Vesoul sticking resolutely to his broken English because, for one thing, he couldn't make out a word that Donald said. Bernard attempted to join in, remarking, 'Quel coincidence' and 'formidarberlay', and even 'pas de chien', though that was no longer true, but they ignored him.

After a while Penny said firmly that some entertainment must be laid on for the boys, at hearing which M Vesoul broke off his war memoirs and announced that they must see the windmill. 'Vair ancient monument, madame. And a beautiful walk up zee liddle path be'ind the 'ouse and through the orchards. I show you.'

The boys enjoyed the walk because the path was thick with the previous autumn's leaves, and because Bernard was so intent on gleaning information from Dick about dogless hotels that he forgot to complain about them ruining their shoes. He also found himself trying to overhear the hushed conversation, in English, between Vesoul and Donald, about the farmer's expected glut of apples. 'I think, 'owever, your Government will buy them. This is big country, France. You do not 'ave room for apples in your island, I think.'

'We have marvellous apples, m'sieur.' Bernard was incensed. 'None of your golden delicious rubbish.'

'Oui, m'sieur. They are vairy good, yes?' They arrived at a clearing beyond which stood the windmill on a hillock. Bernard, deciding to be tactful, observed it and, thinking to go one better than Donald, spoke English with a Parisian accent. 'Vair-ree shar-*ming*. 'Ow chic!'

'Oh no, sir. It is *ancient*. So old that we say, in my country, Jeanne d'Arc slept here.'

A winding, wooded road led the Plums the following evening to a lake and the Manoir, recommended by Dick, which was built beside it. Grim stone terraces and steps led down to the water from a five-storey, severely rectangular, brick building.

Dick and Dilys greeted them proprietorially, standing at the top of semi-circular steps, and bowing them in. A pitifully emaciated and grubby cat shot out of the doorway and ran past them. 'There goes your dinner, Tone,' chaffed Dick heartily, and Penny's heart sank at the resumption of pseudonyms. She went upstairs with the boys while Bernard became locked in combat with the patron who, having asked him for his passport, was now attempting to reconcile the name, '*Plum*, Bernard' written therein, with the other name, '*Cupboard*, Anthony' under which Dick Oxenford had booked accommodation for him.

'Cest *Ploom*, n'est pas?' said the patron, who was patron-shaped, with a convex frontage, drooping moustache and a bald pate mostly hidden beneath a beret. He narrowed his eyes to examine the features of his client closely, and looked first at the passport, then at Bernard, again at the passport, again at Bernard. Even allowing for basic ill-will and the usual time lag between photograph and the ravages of nature, he had to admit it was the same man.

'Mais, c'est formidable, m'sieur. Pourquoi, *Ploom*, donc?' He banged the back of his huge hand on to Bernard's passport. 'Alors, M'sieur-er-er-Ossenfort . . . oui?'

'Oxenford, yes.'

'Il a dit que votre nom est, *Cub*-port.'

'C'est mon autre nom, Moose-year.'

'Comment?'

'J'ai les deux noms.' Bernard tried smiling disarmingly, thinking of Chaplin in a similar plight, but he failed to charm the patron who looked ever more hostile and demanded, 'Vous avez un nom-de-plume?'

Bless the old bugger, Bernard thought. 'Oui, Moose-year. That's it. That is exactly it. *Ploom*, c'est mon nom-de-plume. *Ploom* et *Plume*.' He fell about, as did not the patron who narrowed his eyes even more venomously and enquired why the nom-de-plume was the name written in the passport.

Glibly, Bernard said that was the law in England, adding, 'Bientôt, Moose-year, dans le marché commune, c'est le law ici, aussi. Aussi, ici.' The Patron stared at him unbelievingly, then looked at the passport again, shrugged his shoulders and said, as he waddled away, opening a door into the service quarters with his convex frontage, that the British should never have been admitted to the E.E.C. He had always been a Gaullist.

'J'agree, absolutement. C'est un farce bureaucratique.' Relieved, nonetheless, Bernard rejoined his wife. 'We may all be had up with conspiring to forge documents.'

'Have we forged any?'

'No, but I mean with pretending to be forged documents.'

'Are you pretending to be a forged document?'

'Ya!' Bernard sat down on an extravagantly large chaise-longue and examined the room which was twenty feet high and covered with lurid, brocaded paper. Every square inch of it, and of ceilings, doors, cupboards, skirting-boards and shutters, had been daubed with paint and paper, and in the room were three double beds, four vast wardrobes, two escritoires, several chairs and an expansive round table resting on one central and wobbly leg with five arched feet. The bathroom was adorned, across an area of black-and-white tiling the size of a small piazza, with a deep trough into which water could be gushed by operating stiff, archaic taps. In the passageways were complicated systems of hot and cold water pipes, lagged here and there, giving the impression of a ship's engine room.

The loo, in contrast, dejected Bernard. Its type had once been altogether too common and he had wrongly supposed it now to be extinct even in the depths of rural France. He crouched unhappily above an aperture in the porcelain square, his legs stretched before him to protect his dropped trousers from contamination. He helped himself to several sections of paper reminiscent of that used for printing wartime novels. There was limited space between himself and the latched door. By his right hand was a chain to operate the flush. He stood to pull up his trousers but found himself then unable to reach it. He leaned back acrobatically, tugged at the chain with one hand at the same time as releasing the door catch with his other and, as a mild spray hit his back, jumped out on to the landing directly into the path of a correctly dressed man who half-bowed and said coldly, 'Pardon, m'sieur.'

'Non, non, je me pardon, Moose-year. La deluge! Ma fois!'

The Frenchman bowed again and entered the loo.

'Passage non protégé,' bellowed Bernard.

The dining-room was even more magnificently equipped than the bedroom and the bill was correspondingly

Hiltonian, which was a determining factor in their decision to leave at crack of dawn, and breakfast cheaply at a café, before proceeding to Murville-les-Fagots where Dick had recommended 'an exquisitely run-down hovel on the banks of the sometimes pathetically trickling Poivre'.

At 23, The Spinney, Ikin Copse, the Longhorns' Sunday ritual with the newspapers was in full swing. The magazine section of one publication had so enraged Adrian that he was using it, instead of the automatically despised business section, to make his paper darts.

Tina, picking up the *Gazette*, said, 'Oh, I remember that. Wasn't it nice, dawling?'

'Where's that?'

'St Martin-sur-Cadeau. The farmhouse with all those gorgeous alsatians. *The first of a new series*,' she read out, '*about little-known French country hotels far from the madding*.'

'Not now they've got hold of it.'

'Lucky we've been there already.'

'We'll always be a few jumps ahead,' said the Lecturer in Modern French History at the University of Ware, lunging at his wife and flicking at her nipples with his index fingers. 'Quickly,' he shouted. 'I'm gasping for my coffee.'

The door bell chimed out a Vivaldi theme.

'If it's those bloody property people again don't open it, Tina.'

After leaving the Manoir they drove for an hour down minor roads with frequent signs warning them of *Chausée deformée* and *Accotement non stabilisé*.

'You might think, dear old dotty things, that they'd find it simpler to re-make the road surfaces instead of littering the verges with these signs. Some of them, I do believe, go back to the *ancien régime*.'

'I just hope,' said Penny, 'that they've stabilised their rives by the time we want to picnic.'

'We'll buy the mon-jay when we stop for les onzièmes.'

'Lay what, Dad?'

'It's wog for elevenses.'

'Bernard!'

'There's a town coming up,' Bernard advised. 'Time for the old petty day-jernay. "Welcome to Frapchaux," it says. "Une ville très ancienne." What's the betting there's a twelfth-century église and ramparts. They're bonkers about ramparts in bloody abroad. Centre ville, here we come.'

'No ramparts,' Donald informed them, 'but it does have a very fine early thirteenth-century church. Two stars in Michelin. If you don't object I shall cast my optics over it whilst you are breaking your fasts. I will wait for refreshment until elevenses.'

Donald, a fastidious bachelor, could not bear to witness the wreckage surrounding the consumption of a continental breakfast. More importantly, he needed to have some time alone to consider how best to get in touch with his friend in Brussels about the scheme he had in mind following his discussion with M Vesoul about apples. It was something he wished to keep private from Bernard, something he must work out by himself. Guided by the church spire, he reached the Place Lamartine where, from a café table placed in the morning sunshine, he commanded a splendid view of the

34

holy edifice, as he sipped coffee laced with cognac.

Meanwhile, inside the Café de la République, uproar reigned as the coffee machine concentrated all its energy on producing the 'deux café-au-lait, *grands*, mais très *grands*, m'sieur' which Bernard had ordered. The machine bellowed, shook and whined, roared, whinnied and fluted, and then, after one long sustained screech in its own approximation to top C, it let out a contented sigh, as old steam engines do after they have come gently to rest at the buffers, and, for a moment, there was peace.

Brian and Simon sucked at the straws in their coke bottles and blew bubbles. A platter of bread and a dish of thin, brittle toast were placed on the table by a cheerfully fatigued waitress. Small pats of butter, individually wrapped in tinfoil, reclined in one dish and sugar lumps, each enclosed in their own paper cover, in another and, dotted about the table, were many circular containers, also of tinfoil, declaring themselves as raspberry or apricot or plum or strawberry jam, but actually filled either with a gelatinous red substance or a gelatinous yellow substance, both of extreme stickiness and tasting of nothing but sweetness.

The Plums broke their bread enthusiastically. Crumbs flew across the table which quickly became surfaced with the remains of the jam containers, butter wrappings and the greaseproof paper which had given protection to the sugar lumps. When Simon requested a cup of tea, the litter was added to by the pyramidal milk holder which he opened inexpertly, pouring most of the contents on the table top, and a swollen teabag which oozed on to the paper tablecloth until Penny, repelled, attempted to sop it up with oily, sticky, strips of tinfoil and finally placed it in the mustard-yellow ashtray generously provided by the promoters of the Lotérie Nationale. But Bernard was not to become disgruntled by a disorder which, in his own home, would have reduced him to quivering rage. He was enjoying himself.

'Lovely coffee. Another cup, dear?'

'I don't think I could endure the noise.'

'Worth it. M'sieur, encore du café, s'il vous plaît. Merci. Regardez le Francaise, Pen. Another coke, Brian? Un autre?'

Once more the din of the coffee machine, engaged in dreaded conflict with itself, quelled all other sounds in the café. Penny applied herself to translating the statutory notice about drunkeness in the République and surprised herself by knowing so many words that she announced she must purchase a better dictionary. Bernard waved her farewell and demanded, 'Encore du cross-onk, s'il vous plaît.'

More metal foiled packages were opened. The boys began to play with them in a desultory way, making tinfoil boats in which pieces of bread were placed to denote sails, and even sailors. The patron, from behind his espresso machine, looked impassively on at the squalid sight. It did not matter to him; it would all be gathered up in the disposable table-cloth and thrown into the garbage. Friends of the earth? Pouf!

Penny, in search of a bookshop, stumbled into the Place Lamartine just as Donald, who had only that moment returned from the café phone booth having successfully made contact with Brussels, was being served his second cognac. 'I felt faint, dear heart, as I was crossing the crossing.'

'What was the church like?'

'Stunning. There's this Romanesque porch, you see, surmounted by a flamboyant Gothic gable, and it opens through the façade . . .' Donald hoped Penny hadn't read the Michelin. 'And you'd adore the groined vaulting. Doesn't groined vaulting send you?'

Back on the road, Penny applied herself happily to her new dictionary.

'So, how do you say "My television mechanic has been struck by blackout"?'

'You are so silly, Bernie, that your postilion would fall off his horse if he heard you. What is so dreadful about my wanting to learn some of the language? It should help us. Don't be insular.'

To illustrate that he was nothing of the sort Bernard pulled up at the next filling station and negotiated with the attendant himself.

'Deux litres,' he demanded, airily.

The attendant looked incredulous.

'Deux litres . . . s'il vous, plaît . . . my man.'

Penny whispered to Donald, 'He thinks he's ordering the wine.'

Bernard said slowly, and icily, 'Deux litres, quatre étoile, s'il vous plaît, m'sieur.'

An awful truth occurred to him.

'Pardonnez-moi, m'sieur. I meant, forty-two. Forty-deux, m'sieur. Ca va?' 'Oui, quarante-deux, m'sieur . . .'

Donald asked Penny, sotto-voce, 'Why does he want forty-*two*, anyway?'

'Something to do with the conversion.'

'If he's ever converted, dear heart, I shall become a fuzzy-wuzzy, I promise you.'

'Can't call me insular after that,' said Bernard, driving away.

'Let me test you on a few words. You're doing so well, darling.'

Bernard allowed instruction to take place until the matter of the article cropped up. 'Don't give me all that le and la business. It can't possibly matter.'

'It's to do with the structure, dear heart, of the language.'

'Time they got rid of it. Le this, la that, what a daft habit. Now that we're in the common market I hope we'll abolish it, along with their rubbishy apples. We'll go in here. Lovely spot.'

Bernard suddenly lunged off the road into a field littered with plastic bags, beer cans and cow pats.

Donald hated picnics but maintained an air of dogged sang froid. He was determined never to appear ill at ease in this country to which he felt so spiritually and culturally attached, and especially not in front of the philistine Plums, which was how he thought of them. Yet, seated on a surface of ant hills beside a river bank, trying to spread butter and pâté on to a crusty portion of loaf, at the same time as not contracting cramp in his calf muscles, was not congenial for an unathletic man of sixty plus. Nor did he care overmuch to drink what was an admittedly very passable plonk, bought at the local Economique, out of a bakelite beaker. To establish superiority, and maintain his role as civllized traveller and connoisseur-extraordinary, he said, 'I see there is a little china cup in your picnic basket. It looks almost bone from here. May I have my wine in it, please?'

'By all means, but I wouldn't have thought it mattered as we are only drinking château bottled alimentation-générale.'

'There, Bernard-O, you show your ignorance, I fear. The wine one purchases in these humble market places, for all that it may have been poured into an old brandy bottle, with a plastic stopper, is some of the best we can drink. Do not despise it. And I think I shall savour it best, in my wily wizened way, from a cup.'

'Next time, Pen, don't forget to pack the Waterford glass. Actually it is rather good, isn't it?' Bernard drained his beaker.

'Of course, it wouldn't travel,' mocked Penny.

'It'll travel in me all right. Better watch out for le breathylizer.'

'Or *la.*'

Due to a delay caused by encountering a *convoi exceptionelle* transporting gigantic sections of concrete piping ('I thought they were supposed to go *under* ground, dear hearts') and a confusion over two similarly named towns, Quandres and Candres, only one of which lay on their route – though they visited both – they did not arrive in the outskirts of Murville-les-Fagots until nearly seven o'clock, by which time Donald was feeling car-sick.

On entering the town a large *deviation* notice compelled them to turn left and away from the river on whose left bank they knew their hotel to be situated. They proceeded down narrow streets to areas of former sandy wasteland on which tower blocks of workers' flats had been erected, and then, abruptly, they were heading for open country again.

'You ought to have turned right, Dad, when you went

left.'

'Shut up, Simon.'

'I think he's correct, darling.'

'It doesn't help to have it pointed out.'

'I would have thought it did help.'

'All right. So I'll turn round as soon as I can.'

'You could do a three-point turn, Dad.'

'Now it's "Shut up, Brian",' said Simon.

Bernard executed a rapid manoeuvre, and kept his temper by exercising unusual willpower. 'How maddening it all is. Let's think about something nice. Wonder what we'll have for the old manger, ce soir?'

'Dad?'

'Yes, Simon.'

'This is where we went wrong.'

'Thank you, Simon.'

'Dad?'

'Yes, Simon.'

'We're going wrong again.'

Bernard flung the car suddenly to the left causing a hoot of rage and terror from a moped rider, who had to make his own emergency swerve and shouted abuse in the Englishman's driving window.

'Thank you, Simon.' Bernard hummed a melting melody.

'I do hope, dear heart, you will find the hotel rather quickly. I'm feeling distinctly queasy.'

Penny looked with concern at Donald's unnaturally pale face.

'You ought to carry a flask.'

'It's empty. This has been a long drive, Penny.'

'Diversion ahead,' sang out Simon. 'Dad?'

'Simon?'

'You know last time I said you were wrong . . .'

'Yes.'
'I think I wasn't right.'

'We might settle here for a few days. Seems an attractive place. The old Poivre fleuving by down there.' Bernard looked out of the large casement window at the scene below. 'And I must send in some copy to show I'm actually earning my keep. But first – ah ha! Look at this. It's not bad value at all. We've got our own bathroom and loo despite what that old dragon of a Madame said.' Bernard had opened what he had supposed was a cupboard. 'I shall take a dip.'

He started to turn taps. There was a prodigious rumbling in the pipes and a shower of water sprayed forth, mostly landing on the floor, whilst Bernard wrestled with a lever to divert it through the tap. He succeeded in reducing the volume to a thin dribble but it still escaped via the shower. At length he managed to hold the lever in the tap position and the bath began to fill although the plug remained obdurately open. With the other hand he played with a round gadget which, he supposed, must lower the metal plug into a sealed position if correctly manipulated. But it didn't. (How did people cope with oil spurting up from the ocean bed?)

He turned off the water, undressed, whistled, and ignored the entire ablutionary contraption, as a cat ignores the mouse or ping-pong ball it intends to attack.

Suddenly, Bernard lunged at the bath again, holding the tap with one hand and placing one foot on the plug to hold it down by force. The water gushing from the tap was cold.

Not freezing, but unpleasantly cold, and he looked for another lever to adjust it to hot. This he located hanging from the wall, to which it clung tenuously by a thin shred of plaster. A needle on it pointed at red, which should have signified hot.

It wasn't.

He forced the needle over to blue and the water remained stubbornly cold. He decided to let it run for a while and, allowing the shower to play into the bath, he laid out his washing equipment.

After a few minutes there were violent choking sounds in the pipes and the shower began to splutter boiling water into the bath in short sharp jets. He swiftly re-applied hand and foot to the levers to contain the water in the bath. Scalded, he withdrew them even more quickly. The bathroom had filled with steam. He felt for the control and turned off the water.

He sat on the closet seat calming himself. Then an interesting event occurred. Although he had not touched a knob or tap since turning off the boiling water the pipes again began to rumble and a spout of boiling water shot up from the plug hole.

'This is downright bloody dangerous,' he cried, outraged, as some of the deluge fell on him. He put his foot on the plug to hold it down and withdrew screaming because the plug was red-hot.

Again he retired to the closet seat. And watched. Water continued to rise in the bath to a height of several inches but he became aware that it was less than boiling. He tried it with his hand and found the temperature bearable. He climbed in, felt gingerly for the plug which was now cooler, and clamped his foot down on it hard. A moment later he heard a muffled shout of alarm from what could only be an adjoining bathroom. With some satisfaction he immersed himself and allowed his foot to float away from the plug hole.

After a while he was aware that the water-level was rising, not falling, and that the agitated conversation overheard from the next door bathroom was in German. Then he noticed that the water, although still rising, was becoming colder. He put his foot on the plug again and, again, there was a shout of exasperation from next door.

He decided he had had enough. It was the boys' turn. They would delight in the eccentric plumbing – might even tame it. He got out and began to dry himself but, looking down, observed that the water was still rising. Then, looking down once more, he noticed there was no overflow pipe.

He beat on the party wall shouting, 'Turn off your tap!' Guttural exclamations came back at him. He knew little German but hazarded a bluff. 'Achtung! Die watereisse iss gereissink schnell-strasse! Bitte, offschtoppen die tappenberg.'

There was no response, except from the water which began gently to drip over the edge of the bath. Bernard grabbed his dressing-gown and rushed round to the adjoining suite on the door of which he rapped urgently, shouting, 'Achtung! Achtung!'

A small, fat man opened to him and looked amazed.

'Scusi. Verzeihung, that is. Je suis desolé. Schtoppen die tappenberg. *Die flut*! *Die flut*!'

'Die flut,' said the German, trying to stop Bernard opening the bathroom door for the good reason that his frau was therein.

'Ja, ja, die flut, mein herr. *Armageddonstrasse*!' Bernard sought desperately for the appropriate word. 'The shower. Understand? Douche? Doosher? Ja, *doosher*.'

'Ja, ja, die douche. Frieda, Frieda,' shouted the German and commanded his wife to avert calamity. 'So why you did not say so before? Vat is wrong?'

Bernard explained, the German listened seriously, and thanked him for saving the hotel.

The Madame, who had now arrived on the landing, was not so impressed. They should not, she said, have been using the bath; it was not included in the price of the room. They must pay an extra twenty francs.

Bernard protested that as the bath was not in proper working order, far from charging more for their room, she should charge less.

'Oui, m'sieur,' she replied, with infinite irony, 'peut-être.'

Eventually agreement was reached that the bathroom would not be used again and that there would be no extra charge.

'Ca va?'

'Ca va, madame.'

'D'accord, m'sieur.'

'D'accord, madame.'

'Merci, m'sieur.'

'Merci, madame.'

Bernard wondered if they should all shake hands. Instead he spoke.

'And, madame?'

'M'sieur?'

'Alors!'

'Oui, m'sieur . . .'

'And . . .'

'M'sieur?'

'Donc!'

'Donc, m'sieur?'

'Avec les knobs.'

When they left Murville immediately after breakfast, following a noisy night during which all the youth of the town drove motor scooters along the towpath, Bernard swore that the reception area, which lay beneath their suite, was about to be deluged in his bath water as the ceiling collapsed.

At the next resting place, twenty miles away, up a tributary of the Poivre, all was tranquillity and good will which was as well for the Plums because Simon went down with a heavy cold, and they stayed there for some days.

Recognizing that he shouldn't laze away this period Bernard organized trips to nearby châteaux. Penny accompanied him to Mont Claude where an impressive keep still stood, a magnificent ruin, above the most primitive torture chambers ever designed in the pre-Hitler era. In the adjoining castle, much restored, a guided tour was about to commence as they entered the cobbled courtyard.

They followed a horde of sightseers down spiral steps and through a great hall. A considerate assistant-guide, recognizing foreigners, handed the Plums leaflets. '*Here*,' they read, '*in the anteroom was it that the youngful bride of the Duc de Marmoulian fell first face into the gore of her slained husband.*'

They were hustled down a long corridor leading to a huge chamber which, all having been duly squeezed into it, was then locked and barred.

'La chambre de l'Agnes Sorel,' the guide announced.

'More like the noir hole de Calcutta.'

They were jammed shoulder to shoulder, camera case to small of back, in an interior lit only by a thin stream of sunlight which penetrated the tiny, diamond-shaped medieval window panes, and they stood, one solid phalanx of humanity, plus a yapping poodle or two, while the guide prattled on.

Bernard became aware of being ordered to regard the tapestries, and wished he could. Lingering on the edge of the crowd he at last perceived them, and stopped to gaze as the multitude were bullied into entering yet another unfriendly hall. 'They're really very good,' he remarked to Penny but menacing acolytes urged them on into the next corridor, the next hallowed chamber. Once in, the door was made fast.

'I counted three hundred and fourteen people being squeezed through that last archway. The guide'll retire on what he makes from this.'

Bernard came to regard himself as something of an authority on the Loire châteaux. Contemplating one piece of copy as they drove towards the Poivre on the day before the idyll at the secluded hotel was due to end, he mused aloud. 'I shall say it's as symmetrically perfect as Chambord.'

'You *could* say that, dear heart.'

'Why shouldn't I?'

'Because Chambord – is not – symmetrically – perfect.'

'Everybody says it is . . .'

'You have only to look at it to observe that it is not' Donald launched into an elaborate analysis of the famous château's roofscape, noting a dormer window here but the absence of one on a balancing tower, comparing this spire with that, and so on, and for so long, that Simon wished fervently he hadn't recovered from his virus.

'You might, in your wily wizened way, say "as symmetrically perfect as Cheverny" . . .'

'I might. Except that we didn't go to Cheverny. It was shut.'

'. . . On the other hand, the very fact that the busts on the south wall of Cheverny are unidentical makes this also an inaccurate statement, strictly speaking, though I wouldn't wish to appear to be labouring the point. . .'

Penny was pleasantly surprised as they entered the drive of the Hotel de la Loire at Regency to note terraced gardens with cedars and pines, neatly pruned rose bushes, azaleas and rhododendrons already flowering, and a dazzling display of laburnum.

'I'm going to enjoy this, Bernie darling. You are clever to find such an enchanting place.'

There were three telegrams awaiting Bernard, all from his office, the most urgent commanding him to phone Monty d'Etaing at once on arrival. It was dated four days previously.

Uneasily, Bernard felt he should have stuck to his itinerary, or at least advised his office of his whereabouts during Simon's illness. After he had phoned Monty he was in no doubt at all.

'Never mind where you've been or why. We haven't had a line of copy from *you*, and the opposition's already in print.'

'What opposition?'

'*Gazette*, of course. They already have a man over there who has written up the hotel you planned to stay at the first night.'

'What, St Martin-sur-Cadeau?'

'Yes, wretched Bern, so you needn't bother to tell our readers about that one. Anyhow, they now know its name. The Lord's furious. Taking it personally, so you must phone through copy for next Sunday . . .'

'Right . . .'

'And if you've been to the Manoir de la Flot – '

'We have.'

'Forget it. The *Gazette* has too. And it's been written up.'

'When did the other series start?'

'Two Sundays ago. *He'd* been to the Manoir last year. Why didn't you phone, Bern? The Lord is highly displeased with you. There's a witch hunt on about the leak.'

'Do you mean the series is now current. Not for next year?'

'Yes, for Christ's sake.'

'How was I to know?'

'By tele-bloody-phoning me. Where have you been all your life?'

'I'm sorry.'

'Send in something really startling soon. *Now*!'

'I'll try.'

'Cheers, Bern.'

'Monty?'

'Uh?'

'What's the name of the *Gazette* man?'

'Trafford Clarke. Know him?'

'Don't think so.'

'There's a photo of him with his wife in the *Times*. P.H.S. seems to have something against him. Get a copy. May give you a lead.'

'Sorry, Pen, but we're not staying here after all. Got to get on.' They drove into Blois where Bernard telegraphed his copy through to the *Wanderer* and promised Monty that, henceforth, he would stick to the planned route. He found a newsagent who had just received the previous day's *Times* and turned to the Diary where there was a splodgy photograph of two people standing outside what he could just recognise as the Vielle Ferme de Brieu, but only because the caption told him so. It also named the two indistinguishable figures as Annabelle and Trafford Clarke but that wasn't much help. By then, the only other copy had been sold so he was none the wiser about his rival.

After a tiring all-day drive they approached a hill the other side of which was the valley of the Dordogne.

'Why,' enquired Simon, 'are the hotels we stay at always down country lanes? My schoolfriends stay at seaside places. Why can't we?'

'When this lark's over, we will. On our proper holiday. Look! Birds' nests!'

The boys were duly diverted until Donald remarked, 'That's mistletoe.'

'Birds' nests,' Bernard maintained.

'That's right,' Simon agreed, ever eager to oppose Big-Prick Donald, as he thought of him.

Brian whispered, 'You wouldn't really expect, Dad, to find a bird's nest halfway up a tree.'

'Why not? Jolly sensible place to build it. Not so far to go. Strongest part of the tree.' Bernard sulked momentarily, until they approached a wooded road with hairpin bends. 'Now I can practise my mountain driving. I love this sort of road.'

He was less enthusiastic a few minutes later when he rounded another bend to find himself behind a fifteen-ton tanker dragging its mammoth body ponderously upwards.

'I shall enjoy the view, dear hearts. It's a nice change to go slowly.'

The truck belched out a vile-smelling cloud of exhaust, and Donald reached for his brandy flask.

Woods gave way to fields and hedges on a small plateau at the end of which at its highest point was a hamlet, where a sprawling building stood beside an ivy-covered ruined tower which had been partly restored to allow for a *table d'orientation* at the top.

'The guide calls it "the smiling little village of Dulac". It has a "vue magnifique",' Penny told them.

Simon said he was sick of views. 'And how can a village smile? What a soppy guide.'

They drove past a cluster of houses, a shop, a bar and a church, opposite which was a small communal car park commanding an outlook over mostly deserted, hilly country, rich in vegetation. Simon groaned when he saw it and got under the car rug.

The customary figure, dressed from head to foot in black, greeted them as they walked past the foot of the tower, and were attracted towards a spacious kitchen, with open door, where men and women were eating prior to serving the guests with dinner. But this madame had the smile of a madonna and did not cast any doubt at all on the availability of rooms. She left that task to her husband who, true to form, worked up the usual drama about no room at the inn. Nonetheless, after trudging them all about the little hilltop settlement, visiting this annexe and that, he found them accomodation in 'la grande suite', reached up typical Dordonesque exterior stone steps.

'Voilà!' said M Rostand, proudly, and announced that, when they were ready, Madame Rostand's table d'hôte dinner awaited them. Bernard soon forgot his pre-occupation with trying to work out the identity of his rivals as one superb dish followed another.

Next morning, Penny and Brian having been laid low by the richness of the cuisine, Bernard spent writing copy which he then phoned through to Monty who told him, 'There's a cable on its way to you, telling you to make tracks for Provence. You must out-manoeuvre this bloody Trafford Clarke and start operating in a different part of the country. Get on your way today.'

'Penny's ill too. Monty, does it matter all that much that the *Gazette* is also doing a series? I mean our readership . . .'

'Tell that to the Lord. And the *Gazette* is being shitty about it. Deliberately making fools of us. Give that Trafford the slip, Bern. Find some stunning place he won't recognize. Now, we shan't know where you are, so phone through every day in case anything urgent crops up.'

'I'll get away as soon as I can.'

'Now.'

Bernard hung up. If that was the way the proprietor wanted it then he would just have to cheat. As the rain poured steadily down he spent the day writing sheets of description of imaginary hotels which was certainly, he told Penny, going to make the competition difficult to win.

'I should start applying for other jobs, if I were you.'

By late afternoon Penny and Brian had recovered and, the rain having stopped, they took a stroll in the sunshine. As they returned to the hotel a noisy Renault clattered up the rough drive, throwing up clouds of dust. It stopped, the handbrake was applied savagely, and a triple-chinned, double-paunched middle-aged man stepped out.

'M'sieur Vesoul!' cried Donald, rising from a bench where he had been sipping an aperitif.

51

'M'sieur!' responded the Normandy farmer, a beam of delight on his rosy features. He shook hands all round and explained that Madame Rostand was his sister. 'I come 'ere to do business with my bruzzer-in-law. 'Ow is Bruss-*ells*?' He asked Donald.

Donald winked improbably and placed left index finger theatrically against left nostril.

'Mais oui,' replied Vesoul, shaking his head sagaciously.

The Rostands emerged from the kitchen and there was more furious handshaking plus cheek-kissing.

At dinner the Plums were invited to join the family although Madame Rostand was too busy cooking to sit with them. Vesoul and Rostand told them about their property deals.

''Ere in the Dordogne come many English people, yes? Buying up old farmhouses. And barns. Making theirselves 'oliday 'omes. They buy vair, vair cheap. Is good business for them.'

'And for you, dear heart.'

'We not make much from it, because we say, "why you want buy old ruin farm'ouse with no roof, no floor?" Yes, we think you must be very fool-*ish*. So . . .' with elegant shrug of shoulders . . . 'we say, "we not want, no good to us. Give us cash and no more said."'

'Then underneath the old floorboards with the loot, eh?'

They all laughed heartily, the Frenchmen dimly comprehending Bernard's meaning.

'But then,' Rostand went on, 'one day my wife's bruzzer, M'sieur Vesoul, 'ere, is talking to me in this Dulac where we are living. And there is Englishman from St Al-*ban*, yes? He has bought an old cow-shed for thirty thousand francs. Very happy with it, so M'sieur Vesoul 'e ask 'im, what is like round St Al-*ban*.'

'Because,' interrupted Vesoul, 'there was English soldier from there in 1944, at my farm. And one thing and another this man from St Al-ban know this other man who is in. . . real estate? Property? So, we come to buy 'ouses in villages near St Al-*ban*. And we sell to Americans for big trade delegation. But there is snack . . . snack?'

'Snag.'

'Is snag, yes, merci. We buy this big estate in 'Ertfordshire, and we get all the English people agree to move out. All except one people won't go.'

At this moment Madame, beaming with confidence, ushered in waiters who placed in front of everyone a steaming hash from which arose a mouth-watering aroma.

'Maman!' cried Rostand. 'C'est délicieux.'

'Cher coeur! Mais, c'est la grande cuisine de la Dordogne, n'est-ce pas? C'est merveilleux. Comment ça s'appelle, madame?'

'Le booble-squeak, m'sieur.'

'English soldiers teach 'er 'ow to make in war,' explained Vesoul.

Donald tried to hide his shattered feelings as Bernard returned to the subject of property in Hertfordshire, and Vesoul told him that an English journalist had informed him that every man had his price. When that was reached last house would be vacant. But was vairy expensive.

"Ere 'e come,' said Vesoul. 'Mistair Clarke.'

The man they knew as Dick Oxenford came into the dining room accompanied by the woman they called Dilys.

Bernard rose. 'Did you say Clarke?'

'Yes, m'sieur. Trafford Clarke.'

Furious, Bernard strode halfway across the room to confront the couple.

'Hallo, Tone, nice to see you again.'

'You know perfectly well that's not my name, Trafford.'

'Now, don't get so het-up, Bernie. You're a professional journalist, like me. You know we all have to do these things to one another.

'I wouldn't behave in that double-crossing way to anyone, even you.'

'We all have to please our editors. Right? There's no malice in it.'

There was malice though, early next morning, when the Plums left Dulac. Bernard's last action before driving off was to let the air out of all the tyres of Trafford's car and caravan, and pocket the valves.

'Damn,' he said, as they crossed the Dordogne and he dropped the valves into the river, 'I forgot the spare.'

'Good,' said Tina Longhorn, examining *The Wanderer*. 'They've decided to bring forward their series on secluded and tranquil hotels. They've started today. Where do you think this is, Adrian?'

Adrian, deep into an analysis of class in the home counties which the *Observer* was serving up for the umpteenth time, didn't wish to be disturbed.

'I'm sure we've stayed there, dawling. It's in the Poivre valley. Read it.'

Adrian glanced at Bernard's article. 'Yes, we can get that one. It's the place with the two magnificent cats. Hope they're all as easy.' He returned to the study of class.

'Should have got us to do the series. After all, you do write for the *Sabbatical*.'

'Staff job. Anyhow, I don't have the time.'

Tina turned to the *Gazette*. 'That's odd. They're talking about the same hotel in here. Only they've named it.' Her eye lighted on another page. 'Oh, look Adrian, we're becoming quite notorious. "Hertfordshire academic and his wife refuse to sell their home". That's us!'

As they climbed into the Massif Donald began to lecture. 'And do you know the name of that flower which is rioting all over the houses? We keep seeing it.'

Simon showed his contempt by pulling out his Jennings paperback and sinking below the window level.

'It's called forsythia.'

'Actually, Donald, it's wistaria.'

'I think not, Penny . . .'

'Forsythia's yellow, Donald. Sir had some for our project.'

'Yes well, it's very beautiful.' Donald glared at the wistaria and thought how unsatisfactory children were nowadays.

The boys still feeling some discomfort, the Plums put up at a Routier hotel, modern, featureless but bearable for one night, and set off next day, moderately refreshed, making the road to Le Puy before lunchtime.

Donald renewed his discourse on the wonders of nature, confusing clematis with bougainvillea but ceasing abruptly when the breathtaking view of the city was first glimpsed from the mountain highway. The boys forgot their official objection to architectural appreciation as they walked through the narrow, steep streets to the cathedral. Simon even fell so far short of deliberate iconoclasm as to enquire if there was an ambulatory because, if so, he would like to ambulate. The word pleased him but appealed even more to his great-uncle who said with relish, 'An ambulatory only means a place for walking in, and here there is certainly a cloister in which you can ambulate, but you will probably be more interested in the library where there's a book of great rarity, the Theodulg Bible. A unique survivor of Carolingian calligraphy.'

Simon preferred to ambulate and went in search of the cloister where he found the man they'd called Dick seated against a pillar writing rapidly in a notebook.

Trafford did not see the boy approach and was taken completely by surprise when the notebook was snatched from his grasp and Simon fled swiftly across the cloister garden yelling, 'Scoop!'

Penny said Simon should not have filched the notebook and must return it.

'I was only trying to help. I can never do anything right.'

'We're bound to run into him again. I'll give it back then, Penny.' Bernard's scruples were not as fine as his wife's and he wanted to read what Trafford had written.

'I thought at least I'd get a reward. I shall never ambulate again. It's not worth it.'

Not far from Le Puy the Plums arrived at a house clinging to the hillside. There Bernard was given a message which at least diverted his thoughts from the incident with Trafford, but hardly brought him peace of mind. Firstly, said Monty's telegram, the *Sunday Despatch* was now in the act and running a similar feature to their own and the *Gazette*'s but offering better prizes. The Lord was livid. More importantly, however, would Bernard forget about the gastronomic tour for the moment, and proceed at once to Cagnes-sur-Mer where the International Book Festival was being held, and where a new event had been thrust into the programme. A prize was to be awarded for the most pornographic book of the year and the occasion must be covered. Bernard was the nearest available member of staff.

After lunch the boys were again unwell so Penny insisted that Bernard and Donald must go alone to the Riviera. She would follow by train when her sons had recovered.

But Donald said he was also distinctly below par. He mopped his slightly sweating brow in actor-manager style.

'You mean, you expect me to go off alone without a guide? Thanks.'

'Dear heart, you *are* a journalist . . .'

'I don't mind. I just thought you might feel a responsibility to stay at my side.'

'I should be a burden. If I were well enough . . .'

'It may not be necessary to go before tomorrow, even though they say "at once".'

'I don't want to be rid of you, darling, but I think "at once" can mean only one thing.'

'I'll ring Monty. I don't know a thing about this festival except it's at Cannes. And the telegram's got that wrong. They've spelt it C-A-G-N-E-S. Nor have I ever heard it referred to as Cannes-sur-Mer.'

'Different places, dear heart. Cagnes-sur-Mer lies between Nice and Cannes.'

Bernard went off to the phone over which Monty confirmed, with some irritability, that by 'at once' he did,

57

indeed, mean instantly. The porn award was still three evenings away but certain preliminary work needed to be done, such as finding out the various contenders for the prize, and so on.

'Would it be too much to ask for the actual address in Kine-yer?'

'It'll be signposted everywhere. The French do these things very well, but I do have a phone number. Hold on. While Jean's looking for it there's another thing. The Lord's pretty upset, as I told you. Thinks he's been let down in front of his posh friends, so he's had this idea of taking up one of your recommendations and flying a little party over for the weekend. I suspect there's an ulterior motive but never mind. He's rather gone on that place you've done for next week.'

'Which one?'

'You've called it some soppy name like Le Sel et Le Moutarde.'

'Oh, no!'

'By the way, it's *La* moutarde.'

Bernard pulled out a piece of beard in his agitation. 'Ouch!'

'You still there, Bern? What's the real name?'

'I'll have to look up my notes. I'll phone from Kine-yer.' (Le Sel et La Moutarde was one of his imagined hotels.) 'But listen, Monty, I've had a stroke of luck. Is it too late to change next Sunday's entry?'

'The page is made up.'

'Pity, because I've found Trafford Clarke's notebook and in it is his copy for the week after next. We could scoop them.'

'Nothing is impossible. That's better, Bern. The Lord may forgive you yet. I'll get it taken down right away. Then be on your way to the porn show.'

Bernard felt qualms about using Trafford's copy. Simon had, after all, actually stolen the notebook. Yet it could surely be seen as rough justice? He made a mental note of one or two other items and then addressed the book back to Trafford at his Fleet Street office with a note saying, 'Came across this in the cathedral at Le Puy. Think it might interest your readers.'

The first disadvantage of being alone was the difficulty in overtaking without a front seat passenger to advise. After several near scrapes Bernard settled for the sixty miles an hour which the juggernaut in front, conveying *liquide inflammable*, was cruising at.

A small town announced itself as Langogne, and it was evident that the Langognaise were *en fête* because in the long main street festoons of drably coloured triangular plastic flags were strung from house to house above the road. Inhabitants lounged in doorways chatting idly with lazy, shrugging gestures. No doubt this was related to the inevitable deviation which sent him through two farmyards, advertised as *toutes directions*, along a route so pot-holed that he gave up trying to miss them and concentrated on avoiding a herd of cows which left turds on his bumpers and mudguards.

When he at length regained the main road to Nîmes he realized that, for the first time, he would have to drive in abroad at night. He switched on his headlamps, remembering uneasily that his were white, that he hadn't fitted orange filters over them.

Twenty flashes or so from oncoming cars decided him to stop and fit the filters which lay beneath his luggage in a cavity under the boot. Finding them, however, was as nothing compared with fixing them. The instructions read beguilingly simply: 'Remove the glass on the headlamps and secure the filter around them, tucking in the edges so that they are automatically held in place when the glass is re-secured.' But they were not automatically held in place because they kept flapping out. No sooner had he secured one arc of orange filter than another refused to stay in place. The glass which had been so easy to remove would not go back. The long screw resisted the thread from which it had come and the more he panicked in manipulating his screwdriver, the more recalcitrant it became.

His fury and feeling of inadequacy caused him to treat the filter so harshly that it split. After thirty minutes of unavailing effort he flung the filters to the side of the lay-by and set about refitting the glass without the encumbrance of the celluloid. Fifteen more minutes went by and he had not succeeded. Finally he drove off with one unprotected headlight shining whitely before him. Then he noticed that the other wasn't on at all.

He pulled up at the next filling station to buy a new bulb and get the glass fitted. Taking out his phrase book he threw himself at the mercy of the youth who came to serve him.

This was not a sympathetic youth. It was one at that stage of teenagedom when the world is a sour place, relieved only by the existence of pop and of birds. He was not disposed to be helpful to the foreigner, or even prepared to understand him. When Bernard asked if he spoke English the youth just gaped at him.

'Quelque chose est mal. Avec l'embrayage.'

'Comment, m'sieur? Je ne suis pas mécanicien moi.'

'*Alors*! I – *show* – *you*.' Bernard indicated the lamp.

'A demain,' muttered the youth.

'Maintnong,' pleaded Bernard.

'*Im*possible.' The youth slouched off to serve someone else.

'In trouble, old son?'

Bernard could have hugged the newcomer, to whom he explained his predicament.

'They won't actually run you in for it. But it does upset other drivers. There was a night when I was coming over the Grand St Bernard. Pitch black. Thousands of feet up. Only had white headers. There were some nasty moments, I don't mind telling you. Why don't you shack up for the night? There's quite a decent little Relais down the road.'

'Have to get to Kine-yer by tomorrow afternoon.'

'Easy. Lovely road once you're on the flat. Night driving's not much fun round here unless you know the territory, old son. Chute de pierres, and all that. Not that you can do much about them once they're chuting, eh? I remember trying to dodge them coming down the Grossglockner in a gale. Not nice.' He laughed, self-deprecatingly and then let out a barrage of French at the pump attendant who made sharp reprisal noises. The two of them volleyed away at one another for a few minutes and Bernard didn't understand a word. But he got the impression that his fellow countryman wasn't winning.

'You won't get any change out of this fellow. I can let you have a spare bulb if that's any use.' The stranger kindly fitted it.

'Might see you at Cagnes. Going there myself.'

'Really?'

'Have to meet a certain Lord Proggle. Runs a newspaper.

61

Know him?'

'I work for him. Are you something to do with the porn festival?'

'Good God, no. We're in business together. Matter of fact, I'm one of your shareholders. See you then!' Before getting into his car he felt in the boot and produced a plastic carton from which he drew a hunk of cheese. 'What do you think of this?'

Bernard, bewildered, accepted the offering and ate it. 'Very nice,' he said politely.

'Nothing like market research, umm? Cheers.'

As he tried to sleep, Bernard's mind clicked to a new area of worry. What on earth was he to say to Proggle about Le Sel et La Moutarde? He'd have to find something to fit the description. Hours he should have spent resting, he used up poring over the Guide Michelin in increasing desperation.

In his description of the imaginary hotel he had conjured up, in his own eyes, an establishment in the Jura where he had once stayed. He had referred to its rose garden, and its arbours, and to the joys of breakfasting on the terraces, and to the quietly spectacular restaurant which opened into a large round bay, over-looking the river. The trout were freshly caught and the cuisine boasted two rosettes. He knew there was nothing else he had written about which remotely fitted this description. Also he had been mad enough to refer to the proprietors by the actual names of the two who ran the hotel in the Jura – Monsieur and Madame de la Vallière.

He went on fretting long after he had got into bed and was

just about to drop off when he came out in goose pimples all over. He had said it had a private zoo. Proggle had probably chosen it because his friend, the terrible telly-personality animal man, Pilgrim Tolmers, had been invited.

It was an American who, unexpectedly came to the rescue.

Next morning, immeasurably bored by his own company, and with pronouncing every sign and signpost he saw aloud and then translating his thoughts about them into French, he stopped close to Alès to pick up a hitcher. It would help with overtaking, apart from anything else.

'Goin' anywhere near Idalee?' enquired a middle-aged, bronzed man with frizzy hair and a squashed Australian-type face.

'You're pushing your luck. Jump in.'

'I'm Bob Weiss. Noo York teacher on a sabadical. Wriding a book about hitchin' through Europe. You into hitchin'? If I were real lucky you'd turn out to be in a publishin' situation.'

'Do you say that to all your lifts?'

'Sure.'

'Sorry to disappoint. I'm a journalist.' Bernard told him about his mission.

'You're sure into trouble over this Lord. But I reckon I can assist. Little place in the Auvergne I passed through almost fits the description but there wasn't a private zoo, I guess, in the yard, and the proprietors weren't called de la Vallière.'

'That's not vital.'

'And you said there were koala bears in this zoo?'

'What a daft thing to write? Why did I do it?'

'There certainly weren't any in the Auvergne. And the food was real terrible.'

Bernard wished he hadn't picked him up. Bob produced a

harmonica and played well-known tunes. Bernard amused himself by Franglicizing them.

'Nuites et jours, vous êtes the one,
Seulement vous et moi, sous le soleil . . .'

The American interrupted the performance to say, 'I know you're in a hurry but there's a road I planned to take through the hinterland of Provence. Up through the mount'ns from Vaison la-*Romaine*. It'd be just as quick . . .'

'No.'

'You don't want to kill yourself on that modorway.'

'You have no right . . .'

'And I got it!'

'What?'

'I just remembered the hotel you need. It's on that road. It doesn't have a zoo, or koala bears, but it could be the answer to your Lord's prayer.'

'Where is it?'

'Near Draguignan.'

'You win.'

Bernard put his foot down and obeyed Bob's instructions even when, after crossing the Rhône, the American insisted on detouring to Orange because he just had to take in the Roman theatre.

'You into Roman antiquities?'

'I've been there.'

'I just can't live that vicariously. Second left, Bernie.'

After Vaison, they climbed to Carpentras, and Apt, and crossed a high plateau where the sole inhabitant was a

64

disgruntled shepherd. Bob kept up a stream of anecdotes about the country they passed through and Bernard, warming to him, began to have faith in the hotel near Draguignan.

They descended the narrow, highly-hedged entrance into the forecourt of the Hotel Terrasse Ombragée where they instantly noted tables laid out for dinner in the sloping garden. There were roses everywhere, there was a river – a long way off, admittedly, but a river none the less. But there wasn't a zoo. There was, though, an aviary *and* the proprietors were French. Bernard felt his luck had changed and decided they should stay the night and sample the food. Cagnes was only sixty miles away; they could be there by mid-morning.

They showered and changed and went into the small rustic-work bar, decorated in exquisite bad taste. Bob examined the menu and made appreciative comments.

'You really did say that?'

'Say what?'

'Holy mackerel.'

'Sure. I say it all the time.'

'Marvellous. Just like that waitress back in Normandy the first night who actually said, "La, la!" Nature really does follow art.'

'But I'm still waiting for you to address me as "old boy". I'm kinda disappointed.'

'I don't seem to remember what grattons is – or are.'

'Yeah. Got me too. Something to do with grated cheese?'

'Hardly, it's a main course. I bet it's a chicken thing.'

The waiter, overhearing, told them that grattons were pieces of fried pork.

'We're into a real gourmet situation. Can't do justice to this in one sitting.' Bob had ratatouille as a starter and bouillabaisse to follow which Bernard thought a trifle greedy, especially as the other man later demanded a portion of the Englishman's gigot.

'You ain't gonna get through that, Bernie, let's face it. Just give me a taster, huh?'

'May I have a spoonful of bouilla . . . no, it would spoil the flavour.'

'Hmm, not bad. But I'm glad I had what I had. Listen, I should tell you about this guy who put me on to this place.'

'Please do.'

'He's a wrider pal of mine back home. He hasn't broken through yet in a big way but he's had a couple in pocket books. His last one was real funny and the action is set in this actual hotel, where we are sitting now. Although I don't think the owners are aware. I guess we better keep it from them.'

'Why's that?'

'Well, pard of Idaho's theme . . .'

'Idaho?'

'Idaho's his name.'

'He's called *Idaho*?'

'You're real quick, Bernie.'

'Well, why not? Tennessee Williams, after all.'

'Pard of his theme is the cute idea this restauradeur has of popularizing his liddle country establishment. His way of doin' this is to spread it about that he fixes all his most pricey dishes with an aphrodisiac. Makes the perfect plot for someone like Idaho who's not at all shy of putting all the ingredients into his wriding; same as M Cordon-Noire, his chef, does into his cooking. It's bin quite a stir in the States.'

'His hero's called M Cordon-Noire?'

'Yeah. Satirical, huh? I guess it's corny but Idaho's the sort of guy who says to himself, "O.K., O.K., I'm a wrider, so

what do I write? What the public wants, buddy." He doesn't
have complications culture-wise as we would. Just wants to
be in a money situation, and famous.'

'And the man who owns this place doesn't mind Idaho
using his hotel as a peg for the novel?'

'You're real green, Bernie. That's what's so nice about you
Anglo-Saxons. *He doesn't know*. And I guess he wouldn't
care to because he's bent on making this joint real classy.
Wants to attract the jet set up here from the coast.'

'He deserves to after the meal we've just had. The Lord's
lot will lap it up. I must thank you, Bob. It was an act of
providence picking you up this morning.'

'You're welcome.'

In Ikin Copse there was some consternation at 23, The
Spinney. Neither Tim nor Adrian could identify the hotel
which had so taken Lord Proggle's fancy.

'The only place I can think of remotely resembling it is
that nice rambling old shack in the Jura – we stayed there
coming back from the Engadine.'

'But it didn't have a zoo, dawling.'

'No, it didn't. He's got me this time.'

'Do you know this Plum man, Adrian?'

'Why should I? I just drop in to pick up the odd book.
There's an awful lot of people at the *Sabbatical*!'

'Are they all awful?'

'You know what I mean. Yes, most of them are, actually.
What's the *Gazette* man on to this week?'

'He's in the Doyng-doyng. That tiny place on the hilltop

where the patron owns the whole village.'

'Dulac, hmm. Pity he's done that. I should like to have gone back. Mind you, it was getting pretty slummy last time we were there. Half of Hampstead in the place.' Adrian yawned, picked up a supplement at random and was soon engrossed in an article by an American sociologist on the British malaise.

'I don't feel like coffee this morning,' said Tina, screwing up a whole arts section and flinging it over the balcony.

Adrian didn't hear her, and she had to tug his arm rather roughly before he attended to her.

At Cagnes Bernard ran up the wide, dazzling marble steps of the Palais des Expositions thinking, Smiling Big Town by the Beautiful Blue Med. He was confronted by Monty d'Etaing who enquired brusquely where the hell he'd been.

'Car broke down on a mountain road. Good to see you. Is the scepter'd isle still sinking slowly into the North Sea oil bubble?'

'Very funny. I've been worried about you. That's why I'm here. We can't afford a slip-up on this dinner for himself and friends.'

'There won't be any slip-up, Monty. Where's the porn function?'

'Here. Eight this evening.'

'Then there's plenty of time. I've found a marvellous place for dinner, tomorrow. It won't take long from here . . .'

'No matter, he's bringing his private plane. They'll fly there.'

'No can do. It's quicker to drive. The nearest airport is further the other side than we are here.'

'Well, where precisely is this Le Sel et La Moutarde?'

'I'll explain everything. Where are you staying? And if you're here, why am I?'

'It was time we had a chat. And I've got fresh instructions for you. You have to go to Italy next.'

'I do?'

'I thought you wanted to go to Italy. You're back in his good books after that Trafford scoop. He almost smiled when I told him.'

'That's a relief. But just at this moment my family is marooned in the Massif Central.'

'We'll get them out.'

They went back to the car and Bernard explained about Bob. At the hotel, overlooking the Mediterranean, the first person they ran into was Trafford Clarke.

'Hello there, Bern. I think your series is great. Between us we're certainly doing fine things for the French travel trade.'

Bernard decided to play it equally cool. 'My son found your notebook. I sent it to the Press Council.'

'How kind. I had a carbon anyway.'

'Where's Annabelle?'

'She had to go back home. One of those little female things, but she'll be O.K. How are Penny and the kids?'

'Resting in the Massif. Be down in a day or two.'

Bernard added, nonchalantly, 'What shitty work are you up to here, then?'

'Don't be like that, Bern. Come and have a drink.'

'I have my editor with me.'

'Sorry. See you later.'

'Who was he?' asked Monty.

'That bastard is Trafford Clarke. I suppose he's covering

the porn show as well.'

'What a surprise he's going to get at the weekend. I must say, Bernard, I think the stuff you've been sending in is a lot better than his. You seem to have a feel for this job. There's a lightness of touch in your copy that just doesn't come through in his.'

'How very generous of you, old boy.'

'He said it! He said it!' Bob was ecstatic.

'The only thing that natters me,' Monty continued, 'is this character who is sending in stuff to the *Despatch*.'

'Why?'

'It also is very good, and full of natural history on the side, which is probably very appealing to their readers. You know how mad everyone is now about nature since we started concreting it over?'

Monty pulled out a *Despatch* and showed Bernard a column where he read about the gratuitous nature lessons forced upon anyone with eyes to notice as they travelled in search of food and seclusion in France. There was something familiar about the style.

At the end of a day during which the boys had been especially trying, pedantically demanding the exact meaning of everything she said and asking, 'Why?' a thousand times, Penny, having hopefully settled them in bed, walked resolutely towards the bar. It might or might not be the custom for unescorted ladies to use bars in provincial France but she was past caring. Even Donald was not to be found, though she had no special desire for his company unless it was the passport to a strong drink.

Where did Simon get that regrettable characteristic from, that habit of innocent questioning guaranteed to drive any mother to the verge of infanticide? Perhaps from Bernard who, she had to face it, could be unbearably maddening. It was a good job she loved him but he must watch out. There *were* other men.

One such was watching her at that moment with every sign of appreciation as she stood listlessly before the bar engrossed in her uncharitable thoughts. Smiling with dazzling molar perfection, and making an unnecessary adjustment to the fit of his exquisitely tailored suit, he said, in English with a strong Neapolitan accent, 'Barman is not here, madame. I think he putting cows to bed. You know? This is rural France.'

'Obviously you're not French, monsieur. What contempt you have for them.' Penny thought appreciatively, he's noticed I'm a woman, he thinks I'm attractive. Which I am. When did Bernie last look at me like that?

'Is the privilege of next door neighbour. I am Italian. Woppo, you say.'

'I would never be so rude.'

'Even about the French?'

'They are our next door neighbours, also.'

'Touché, as they say.'

A barman appeared, attired in a striped shirt, newly laundered, and finely-pressed blue linen trousers. No whiff of the cowshed on him.

The Italian offered Penny a drink which she accepted, already thinking they might dine together. Which would be something, after this sodding awful day. She no longer cared about what had happened to Donald.

Il Signore asked, 'Do you come here often?' and then

explained that neither did he. He was on an investigation for his Rome-based newspaper. A rumour had been heard that a food mountain of some sort, declared surplus by the common market commissioners, was on the point of being sold to the communists.

'Why does that bring you *here*?'

'My editor thinks for the sale negotiations go here – hereabouts, yes? All day, I am in Le Puy. Find out nothing. There is festival there and I cannot get hotel. I come here. And here I have some success . . . apart from delightful chance of meeting you, Madame . . .?'

'Plum. Penelope Plum.'

'Pen-el-o-pe?' sang the Italian. 'Most classical of names.'

'And yours?'

'Leonardo – Giovanni – Dino-dino – Caradente-Vecchio.'

'And for short?'

'Dino.'

'What was the success you had, Dino?'

'I look at letter rack at hotel desk, and in it is letter for Darien Avonbury.'

'That was good?'

'I think so. This Darien Avonbury is a deputy. A member of parliament, you say.'

'M.P.'

'So. And he is businessman. Has many companies. I think you have a saying. "He has many caps in the fire"?'

'I don't think so.'

'Yes, truly. Means, he does many things. Diversifies.'

'I think you mean he doesn't have all his eggs in one basket.'

'I think so, Signora Plum.' Dino was bewitched.

Penny yawned, unable to control herself. 'My husband will be most interested. He's a journalist, like you.'

72

'He is here?'

'No, he's gone to Cagnes.'

Dino almost laughed his relief.

'And I must go to my children.' Penny was aware of Dino's bedroom eyes and realized she had been flirting too much. Not that that would have made much difference because it was well known that all Italian males imagined all females, Italian or otherwise, to be violently in love with them. But perhaps she had been indiscreet. 'It's been so nice, Dino. Thanks for the drink, and your company. It would have been miserable drinking alone. Especially as Donald hasn't returned.'

'Your husband? You expect him?'

'No, Donald's my uncle.'

'I see you to your room.'

'The lift's over there.'

'I come in and make sure the maid has done the bed properly.'

'No,' she said, 'If she hasn't, the children will help me.'

Dino walked back along the corridor disconsolately. How could you make love to a woman when her children were in the room?

He would have felt more aggrieved had he known they weren't.

The organizers of the Cagnes-sur-Mer International Festival of the Book had sought for some years for a means of popularizing the event among the international publishing fraternity which, for all their efforts, remained obstinately loyal to Frankfurt-upon-Main, where a trade fair was held every autumn with increasing support from all over the world. A few of the hordes who visited Frankfurt annually looked in on Cagnes for tax reasons and spent a day or two on the beach, yet, for the most part the Cagnes Festival was attended by French publishers and a few specialists from the U.K. The West Germans, on principle, would have nothing to do with it and the Italians, with their own Riviera coast, albeit in a more advanced state of desecration, boycotted it, because their tax officials did not recognize it as an allowable expense.

Hence the Pornography Award, which had attracted a number of New York publishers for the reason that no less than three of the books short-listed were by Americans. Of the others, one was French, one German and one Swedish. An official of the British Council, attending the Fair, admitted to a deep sense of shame that his country was not represented and, when invited by a radio commentator to enlarge upon this view, he said, in a voice thick with emotion, that there had been twenty-seven British books entered for the award, against eighteen American and only eight French. What, he would like to know, was wrong with British porn?

The German item on the short list dealt with the night life of Hamburg in the Thirties and was so ponderously symbolic that Bernard found it difficult to locate the dirty parts, but he had only one afternoon in which to skim through all six books. In both the French and the Swedish entries there was a surfeit of lashing and strapping on to beds, interlarded with prolonged philosophical argument about the value of flagellation.

The first American contribution was concerned with a morosely sick gent who used the motor cycle as a sex symbol, and planned to have an orgasm as he crashed into Princess Grace's horse-drawn carriage outside the casino at Monaco. The second described the dark thoughts and deeds of an ex-president who had retired to a Pacific island to set up an Ocean Sado-Masochism Colony for coloured spastics. He had read no more than the blurb of any of these when Bob knocked on the door crying, 'Hey guess what? Who'd you think I met on the sidewalk?'

'Who?'

'Idaho. He's into the porn contest, but he reckons he won't be into a winning situation because the other books are much muckier.'

'They certainly scrape the depths. After just dipping into them I feel I need a shower.' Bernard began to undress.

'Whether he wins or not, there's already a great deal of interest in locating the hotel where the book's set. There's some English journalist bent on findin' out. Think you were talkin' to him.'

Bernard stopped undressing and sat on the bed. He said, 'I'll make a deal. My paper want me to go to Italy after this junket is over. You want to go to Italy, right? I'll take you but first you have to do something for me. The Lord Proggle comes out tomorrow and we take him up to Draguignan. I want you to make sure that Trafford Clarke goes elsewhere. A long way, elsewhere.'

Bob meditated only momentarily. 'Would it madder if I appeared I was radding on you?'

'Do it anyway you like.'

'O.K. Leave it to me. I always fancied myself into a cloak and dagger situation.'

Bernard picked up the last of the six books. 'Is your friend's book called *Cordons of Blue*?'

'That's it.'

'Why's he call himself Catullus Twain Eliot?'

'He reckons it's more classy than Idaho Brown.'

The Porn Award was made in the Conference Hall of the Palais des Expositions.

The panel of judges comprised a notorious international criminal who had made a name for himself as a television commentator on social affairs, so that he now found it both convenient and lucrative to go straight; the owner of a chain of sex markets in Copenhagen; an English lord who had fought his way to the peerage via the trades union movement and the Labour Party; and a Goncourt-winning member of the Académie Française, the eminent poet-philosopher, Davide de Loyale, who was chairman.

De Loyale was author of *La Sagasse Absolument* and *L'Idéal et L'Espère*, both of which were set books at all progressive universities. He had been expected to win a Nobel for the last fifteen years, and still hadn't made it. He spoke at length, mostly in French, but riddled with quotations in German, Arabic, Hebrew, Latin, Greek, New Testament Greek, Rumanian and, even, English.

Bernard could not get the gist of it all but supposed he was on the right track because every so often de Loyale picked up one of the short-listed books, held it aloft during a long peroration, and then dropped it contemptuously into a large waste bin at his side, drawing, as he did so, rumbles of disapproval from the supporters of the candidate he was evidently dismissing.

At last, only Idaho's book remained on the table in front of de Loyale, and the hall hummed with expectation. There came a final crescendo of comment from the distinguished chairman. Then, playfully, he went to throw *Cordons of Blue*, also, into the bin, but, at the last moment, he retained hold of it.

Cordons had won and Idaho was summoned to the platform to receive a cheque for 30,000 NF. He was also invited to comment, and his speech was a relief to Bernard, as well as many others in the hall who were not familiar with German, Arabic, Hebrew, Latin, Greek, New Testament Greek and Rumanian, but who did have a glancing acquaintance with English.

Idaho, wearing an electric blue suit of crimplene, with extravagantly wide lapels and bell-bottomed trousers, radiated good humour. He held up his hand to stop the applause and shook his head very slightly to express disbelief that this could be happening to him.

Lit-er-er-chure meant everything to him, he told them, and he had never imagined he would be so honoured in this world. Many people back home might think it a dishonour to win a prize for pornography but he was elated because he believed, as he thought everyone in the hall believed, that porn was an art, the true, creative expression of the late Twentieth Century. And if he had had an edge over his competitors he thought it was because he hadn't neglected another great art. That of gastronomy.

In blending lit-er-er-chure and gastronomy he reckoned he'd extended the boundaries of credibility, in the interest of art and, also, of religion. Though he didn't claim to be another Mohammed, another Buddha. No sir.

Idaho supposed that folks would be asking if he intended to reveal the name of the hotel on which he had based his fictional hostelry, where so much of the action in the book took place. Well, he guessed, he'd have to disappoint because there never was one single hotel he had based it upon. He had used his knowledge of numerous hotels right across France. There wasn't no prototype.

'So, I'd like to scotch that one at the outset. I don't want folks goin' around sayin', "That's the hotel in *Cordons of Blue*, that's the *Cordon Noir*!" Because you ain't goin' to find it, buds. It don't exist.'

Later in the evening, Trafford Clarke badgered Idaho, unwilling to concede that he couldn't buy the information he needed.

At this point Bob took over and invited Trafford to his hotel room where they were seen, and heard, on the balcony, in intense discussion for nearly an hour.

Bernard had three final cognacs with Monty, who was delighted to know that the hotel to which Proggle and his guests were to be taken was the actual one in *Cordons*, whatever the author might say. He was pleased to be so much in favour at headquarters, especially as Proggle would be commanding his presence some time the following morning. He had hardly reached his bedroom before Bob knocked and entered, 'sideways', as he put it.

'I reckon it'll be sewn up, Bernie. Better not be seen with you again.'

Bernard congratulated him and passed over a wad of bank notes. Alone, he brushed his teeth, drank some Evian water, thought self-pityingly of Penny, and made his way to bed . . . and to the mosquito which attracted most of his conscious attention for the next eight hours.

Arthur Proggle sat on the balcony of his sun-drenched hotel, seemingly admiring what remained of the natural beauty of the Riviera coastline where a four-lane highway was being constructed. What mostly absorbed him was the satisfaction he felt at being Lord Proggle, of High Brooms and Sarratt, taking a brief vacation with personal friends of high rank, linked to the dissatisfaction which ate into his soul that he was not a duke or prince, a cut, that is, above other press barons. It also galled him that his mother, Mrs Gladys Proggle, known as the Dowager, who had nurtured him during her penurious widowhood and seen him through grammar school, and who now queened it over his various residences in Regent's Park, Corfu, Montigo Bay, the Costa del Sol, and Amersham, Bucks, had not received preferment.

Proggle wasn't married. The Dowager Gladys had seen them all off, and it was assumed amongst his acquaintances (Arthur didn't actually have friends) that he was a repressed homosexual with a mother fixation.

Nonetheless, the gossip writers were about to be rewarded because Proggle, at 60, had designs on a young painter, Fauna Wynyates, one of the party invited to Cagnes. She was to be the subject of discussion when Bernard and Monty were ushered on to the Lord's balcony, where the protector of press freedom was pouring himself a further cup of camomile tea.

'What – ah – time, we start then? And how – ah – far this place?' Proggle demanded, it not being in his way to utter the commonplaces of social greeting.

'Good *morning*, Lord Proggle,' said Bernard. 'I hope you are flushed with good health.'

Proggle glared, and waited for replies to his questions, with the air of one about to send for burning pitch to be poured over his adversaries.

'I suggest, Lord Proggle, your party leaves about five, so that they have time to look round the gardens and take cocktails before dinner at eight. The hotel is close to

Draguignan.'

'It better be – ah – good, or I'm warning you, Plum. Your series will be – ah – out. An' listen. I've got er – artiss friend with me. Want her to illustrate the places you – ah – write about.'

'Surely that will defeat the object . . .'

'*Shuddup*. This er – artiss friend is very talented. She can help the series, make people more interested in it all. You'll meet her at dinner. Make sure you say her – ah – paintings are good.'

Bernard tried to look submissive.

'And make sure I get my diet on time. I don't want to wait half-hour while – ah – everyone else is eating.'

Lord Proggle was a vegetarian because he thought he could cheat death for longer by pursuing that course. (Secretly, he thought he would be the first immortal.)

Bernard asked the name of the lady artist. Proggle glowered. He didn't like subordinates to ask questions. Ignoring the enquiry, he stood up and looked over the balcony.

The interview had ended.

Bernard and Monty took coffee together at a café near their employer's hotel.

'Who's this oiseau then? He's never had a girl friend before.'

'The artist. He told you! We're lumbered with her.'

'What's the point in illustrating articles when the whole series is based on people having to guess where the places are? They might well recognize them from Proggle-bird's drawings.' (Also, Bernard reflected, it would make it difficult to invent places.)

Monty wondered if he were supposed to attend the dinner.

'If you're not, could you do something about getting Penny and the boys down from the Massif? I am commanded to attend upon the Lord.'

They were joined by a young man in a plaid-patterned linen jacket, flowing cravat, and beige cord trousers. 'Hi, Mont, over here for the porn show?'

'Bruce! How jolly to see you. Are you covering this? Bruce Drax, Bernie, of the *Chronicle*. What are you – Paris correspondent? Bruce, Bernard Plum.'

Bruce and Bernard shook hands after this complicated introduction, during which the newcomer responded with, 'Hi! No, I'm Western European editor now. Big deal. Aren't you doing that series? But I'm still based on Paris.'

To which Bernard replied, 'Think we met at the Press Club once. Yes, do you like it? Nice to meet you. Must be pleasant living in Paris.'

After that, by tacit agreement, they spoke in turn, and Bruce announced that he had the low-down on the real hotel in *Cordons*.

Bernard looked ahead impassively but Monty, with more sophistication, smiled, saying with great suavity, 'I have the author's personal assurance that there is no such hotel. It is based utterly and absolutely on his imagination.'

'Don't you believe it, Mont. And I'll tell you who knows. That's Trafford Clarke. Know that swine?'

Bernard said he was working on him.

'Are you? Well, he's on to something, as usual. There's some American pal of the author who has leaked it to him,

81

and they're driving off this afternoon to case the joint.'

'Why did he tell *you* all this then?'

'He didn't. I overheard it from my balcony. He and the Yank were there below. Never ever confide anything to anyone on a balcony in Cagnes.'

'So, you're inviting us to join you on a trip to track Trafford?'

'Why not? You don't come out till Sunday. Can't scoop us. And it's important to have someone with me to keep Trafford's car in view. Case I lose sight of it.'

'Pissy-eyed monster. Bern, this Mr Drax is truly resourceful. Why doesn't he work for the Lord?'

'Hallelujah! But we can't join you, Bruce. Proggle has issued a royal proclamation. I have to attend his banquet tonight in full regalia.'

'You'll look cute in a coronet. Mont?'

'I have to be around in case he invites me as well. But good luck with your researches.'

'Oh, I'm on to a cinch. Your Proggle will be so livid.'

'He usually is.'

Penny was distraught when Bernard telephoned. She was running short of money, the children were bored and Donald had disappeared. She thought it best not to mention Dino. 'Donald just left a note saying he was visiting friends and not to wait for him.'

'What's he up to?'

'He was looking very pleased with himself whatever it is. It's something to do with Brussels.' I wonder she thought, if

he's mixed up in this food mountain thing Dino mentioned?
'But when are you coming back, darling?'

'I'm not. There's a car coming for you tomorrow.'

He felt better having made the decision, and passed the responsibility to Monty who paid over thousands of francs to a car-hire firm and despatched a gleaming bronze Renault-16 towards the Massif. 'Beside the bill for tonight's meal at Draguignan,' he said to Bernard, 'the cost will be petty cash.'

Bernard sorted out Proggle's secretary who had taken several dozen phone messages and cables for her employer since his arrival in Cagnes. None of them was of any urgency but Proggle became apprehensive if he didn't receive constant messages from his numerous minions.

'Any directive for me?'

'You are to bring your car round here, Bernard, and give a lift to anyone who needs one.'

'I don't have to drive his lordship then?'

'No. He's hired a vast Merc and most of the company will travel in that, including, no doubt, little Miss Daub.'

'What's her real name?'

'Probably, Doris Jones, But she says Fauna Wynyates.'

'Any talent?'

'Her painting, I can't tell. But for knocking Proggers right off his pedestal, yes. He's absolutely terrified of her.'

It was not apparent as the mogul assembled his guests that he was terrified of anyone. Just servile.

Bernard was fascinated to watch his employer behaving

with the deference of a uniformed chauffeur towards his five guests, one of whom he recognized as having met on the road from the Massif. He received a patronizing nod of recognition and a shouted, 'Got here then. Any more trouble with your lights old son?'

A blonde of indeterminate age slunk up to him and said, 'You must be Bernard Plum. Must talk to you, darl, about the Italy thing. Arthur, I'll go in Bern's car. Can't wait to hear his plans. I'll ride in the Merc coming back, Arthur. With you, darl.'

Proggle blushed. 'You take Miss Wynyates, Plum. She's the er – artiss, I told you about.'

Once in the car on the way to the Hotel Terrasse Ombragée, Fauna, a small, lean lady with slit-shaped eyes and tiny brown pupils, said, 'You must save me from that monster, darl.'

'My bread and butter. Why are you working for him if you feel like that?'

'My art, darl. Must get it published. I'm thirty-one, and I haven't got *any* where. I do draw so well. They all say so.'

'What exactly has the Lord promised you?'

'That my drawings shall illustrate your column, darl. You don't mind?'

'Who am I to mind, if that's the way he wants it? I suppose you can always do surrealist stuff so that the hotels are not recognizable.'

'Never mind the art, darl. You know what we really have to do in Italy?'

'You tell me.'

'There are these missals . . .'

'These what?'

'You know what a missal is. Sort of book of prayers. Things Catholics use. For mass. And these are very special ones. They're inconcubines, or something.'

'Incunables. Books printed before 1500.'

'Daresay you're right, darl. But these are very special ones because they have pictures in them. Illuminated whatsits.' She tugged at Bernard's arm. 'Do wish you'd look at me sometimes.'

'More important to watch the road.'

'I'm not used to safe drivers. Don't have them in Italy.'

'So what do we have to do about these missals?'

'Find them.' She put her right arm through Bernard's left and he extricated himself instantly.

'Prig.'

'When we go to Italy, I should warn you, as you are proposing to share my car, that my wife and two sons will be passengers.'

Fauna pouted.

'So tell me about the missals.'

'I told you. They're lost. Know a woman called Freda Mock-Templeton?'

'I haven't had the pleasure.'

'She knows all about these inconcubine things. She's on holiday in Italy. We have to find her.'

'Why are these missals so important?'

'Not sure. Arthur seems to think they're life and death. I'm surprised he's not more concerned with the cheese. I suppose that's why Darien's here.'

'Darien?'

'Man who spoke to you. Thought you knew him.'

'Tell me more.'

'Daren't, darl. But I don't think the E.E.C. will let them get away with it. Do look at me occasionally. You're the sort who puts ambulance drivers out of work!'

In the garden of the Hotel Terrasse Ombragée, Lord Proggle's guests, who had played at being gastronomes all the way from Cagnes, began to swank in deadly earnest.

'When were you last in Hong Kong then, Darien?' enquired Ted Fountainshorn, once the white hope of the Doncarbonthwaite Constituency Labour Party, now the ennobled chairman of the National Cheese Board, as they were served their first pernod.

'Just back, old son. Opened a new subsid over there.'

'And you really couldn't find *any*where to eat. You astound me.' He held his aggressively handsome head high in astonishment as his face curled into the smile which many found odious but a few alluring, and it was the few who concerned him.

'It would have been bearable if we hadn't touched down at Bangkok on the way, and stayed a night at the Thingy-thing. I suppose that is one of the world's finest hotels.' Darien Avonbury was still in the House but neglected his parliamentary duties to dominate an international corporate which, he privately boasted, paid out more in slush money annually than was allocated to the entire American space programme.

Another guest, Pilgrim Tolmers, remarked that he didn't believe it was really worth discussing the quality of food outside France, to which Bernard replied that he had always understood traditional Chinese cuisine to be unsurpassed.

They gazed at him in silence. Tolmers, who had been designed by nature in a spiteful mood, gazed at him from behind thick lenses and down the length of his almost Cyrano-like nose, as though he were some rare specimen. Despite his bald, pear-shaped head and a posterior that overhung his legs in an ungainly caricature of a stork, Tolmers was utterly self-assured, having a protective pride which led him to suppose that if anyone were normal, which he doubted, it was himself. 'I suppose,' he said, still examining Bernard intently, 'that the most memorable meal of my life was at Perigueux before the war . . .'

Eva, Lady Fountainshorn, romantic novelist wife of Ted, embarrassed, commented vulgarly, 'My most memorable meal is always the one I'm having at the moment.'

Ted, regarding her distastefully, recalled a cassoulet he had once relished at a restaurant in Grasse. 'It was an absolute rondo.'

'I would never,' Tolmers aimed his nose at Fountainshorn to Bernard's relief, 'expect to get first-class cassoulet that far away from the Languedoc.'

A waiter arrived with menus. Whilst they were choosing Fauna asked Proggle if his objection to alcohol was on moral or health grounds.

'Ah – health.'

'You'll do very well here, Arthur,' Ted told him. 'Some of the best vegetarian dishes in the country. Ever tried piscaladière?'

'I go for the simple things, Ted.'

'This is a sort of country tart, dear fellow. Can't get more simple than that.'

'I've never had a country tart.' Proggle looked wistful.

When they were all seated at the dining table, Fauna, in a loud whine, complained, 'Where *does* one eat in the Caribbean?'

'I can tell you. It was in '71. No, Eva, I lie, do I not? It was '70. Noel took me to a little place . . .'

Bernard looked at Proggle to see what he was getting out of all this but he was engrossed in sotto voce talk with Darien. At this moment Donald Ardrake sauntered on to the terrace and sat down at an adjacent table. He waved nonchalantly at his nephew. Proggle, supposing Bernard to be eavesdropping, snapped at him, 'Where's the wine?'

'Oh, I say, Arthur, I've done that.'

'Where is it then, Ted?'

Eva, sensing tension again, asked, 'How's your ratatouille?'

'An absolute rhapsody. Better than the one I had in Aix in '59. No, no, I lie again. '61.'

A Chablis les Clos was served and the waiter, not having been otherwise instructed, poured some into Proggle's glass. Instead of the expected explosion the Lord took a sip, then another, then a mouthful, with every sign of satisfaction.

Ted and Darien exchanged significant looks and Pilgrim took advantage of their silence to relate the details of the second most memorable meal of his life. 'We had this ragoût of snails . . .'

'Cagoule!' bawled Ted. 'An absolute polonaise.'

Proggle shouted at the sommellier, 'Look after my guests.' He then drained his glass.

'How's your piscaladière, Arthur?'

'Delish, Darien.'

'Talking of Franche Comté, as we were, anyone ever had those enormous sausages they eat up there? They call them Jesus.'

'Christ, they don't, Darien.'

'Cook them in water, old son, and serve them absolutely boiling . . .'

'A sort of red hot jazz of a dish.' Bernard drew a disapproving look from Ted.

Proggle rose suddenly and removed his jacket. 'Getting bloody hot. What happened to the – ah – zoo, Plum?'

'Aviary, Lord Proggle.'

'You said zoo in your copy.'

Ever tactful, Eva said, 'Now that you have a taste for the white, Arthur, why not try a sip of red.'

'Do, darl,' encouraged Fauna.

By the time cheese was served Proggle had become drowsy. Ted came into his own proclaiming about a brie which was sheer pizzicato, but recommending that everyone should instantly set off for the Savoy Alps if they wished to savour the grand finale of all cheeses.

'You mean Sassenage, old son?'

'No. Picodon de Dieukefit.'

'I suppose,' Fauna said, drily, 'it's in the Alps where we'd find the cheese mountain.'

Darien changed the subject. 'Isn't it disgraceful about this porn book award? I do think the French go too far.'

'Surely, it's harmless. As a novelist, I think it's rather a good advertisement for books. Not that I write dirty books.'

'Have you read it then, Eva?'

'I have,' Fauna replied for her. 'It's harmless, and rather boring. But I'd like to know the restaurant it's set in. I met a journalist who said he would be revealing it next Sunday . . .'

'The author has assured me quite categorically that there is no single restaurant.' Bernard looked smug and authoritative.

'Point is, whichever, one or many, will the owners be pleased?' asked Tolmers. 'Will they want a reputation for putting aphrodisiacs in their cooking?' He looked piercingly at his host who said,

'Thish one.'

'What one, Arthur?'

'Here.'

'I say, the poor old thing . . .'

'Thish restrong. Thish ish the porn reshtrong.' The Lord

then slumped in his chair.

The group broke up while efforts were made to revive Proggle who was moved close to the aviary to avoid being seen by other diners. A bird awoke and squawked its displeasure.

'Did you get what he said, Fauna?'

'He said it was this place, Eva.'

'Do you think our food . . .?'

Donald, unheeded, completed certain jottings and made for the telephone.

'Ever had chabichou, old son?'

Bernard left them to it, and sought out the gents. Crossing the entrance hall on his return he heard Donald's voice describing the scene on the terrasse. He waited for him to finish and said coolly, 'How were Penny and the boys when you abandoned them?'

'Come, dear heart, they can look after themselves.'

'You were phoning a newspaper weren't you, Donald?'

'I was talking to a friend.'

'You're writing for the *Despatch* aren't you, Donald?'

'My dear fellow, you mustn't jump . . .'

'Did you arrange this before we left home?'

'I've always done a bit of work for them . . .' He laughed nervously. 'I'm not the rich man you always suppose me to be. It's all in investments, which are not doing well . . .'

Bernard thumped him lightly on the upper arm. 'You must have realized it wasn't ethical . . .'

'It's a question of priorities. I wanted to come to France again, and I couldn't afford it . . .'

'It was a rotten trick, Donald, and it'll lose me my job. Find your own bloody way home.'

'I found my own way here, dear heart. I am the navigator.'

Next morning, Bernard was summoned to Lord Proggle's suite and told that he was being held personally responsible for his lordship having become inebriated.

'Not that this would – ah – matter in itself. Disgusting thing to do and won't do it again, ever. *But* – what did I say when I was like that, Plum, what did I say?'

'I shouldn't worry, Lord Proggle. No one will hold it against you . . .'

'I gave away the story of the restaurant, didn't I? Ah?'

'You did mention . . .'

'It's all in this morning's *Despatch*. They've beaten us to it.'

'But it doesn't come out until Sunday.'

'The *Daily* – ah – bloody *Despatch*. Have you forgotten, since you've been over here at my – ah – expense, it's a new daily. I'm – ah – firing you, Plum.'

'That's most unfair. I didn't pour your wine . . .'

'And another thing. Look at this!'

Proggle handed Bernard the *Despatch* which had a brief story on its front page about Proggle and the Chairman of the National Cheese Board attempting to sell the E.E.C. cheese mountain to Rhodesia, through one of Darien Avonbury's organizations.

'You'd never be as silly as that, would you?'

'You're fired.'

'I'll fight it through the N.U.J.'

'Get out.'

With immense satisfaction, Bernard picked up Proggle's cup and dashed camomile tea into his lordship's face.

Bruce Drax, who specialized in overhearing balcony conversations, and who had returned to Cagnes rather disconsolate at losing track of Trafford and Bob, caught some of the drips. A pity there wasn't a photo to go with it but the *Chronicle* carried a front page report next day. Dog wasn't supposed to eat dog but times were hard in Fleet Street.

They were particularly hard for Trafford Clarke. His enthusiastic copy, stating categorically that he had dined at a hotel in the Jura which was the original for *Cordons of Blue*, was sceptically received by his news editor who cabled, 'BLUE HOTEL SITUATED DRAGUIGAN. SEE DESPATCH. SERIES ENDED. YOU REDUNDANT.'

As he drove Monty to the airport Bernard said he supposed he would be eligible for redundancy payment.

'We'll get you home. More than that I can't promise.'

'Will the series go on?'

'Yes. Fauna starts for Italy at once. Your replacement will join her there. You've been unlucky, Bern, but also rather an ass.'

'Thanks. What about the cheese mountain story?'

'He's not saying anything.

'Bound to be questions in the House.'

'Leave that to Darien Avonbury. The latest Member to have a retarded bright future.'

At the airport they met Donald who drew Bernard aside.

'I realize, dear heart, I have behaved extremely badly. I want to make it up to you.'

'So?'

'The *Despatch* is not going on with its series but the other people are.'

'What other people?'

'The *Gazette*. They asked me to take over from that dreadful Trafford person who was so horrid to you. He's been sacked also, you see.'

'Why are you going home then?'

'I turned it down. And I suggested you. You'll be hearing from them.'

'Donald, that's very good of you.'

'The least I could do, dear heart. Forgive me. My flight.'

Bernard didn't notice that Donald's destination was Brussels.

The phone rang at 23, The Spinney, before the Longhorns had woken up. Adrian climbed wearily and crossly from bed and staggered down the long staircase.

'Monty d'Etaing here. *Sunday Sab*. Wonder if you can help us out of a spot. You know that series we're running on tranquil hotels in France . . .?'

'I do.'

'No one needs to tell me what an expert you are, Adrian . . .'

'Oh, I don't know . . . But as a matter of fact, it would be frightfully convenient. We've just sold this house and we're putting our things into store . . .'

Part Two

'Graatzieh,' said Bernard, sounding as though he were tearing a strip of emery paper apart, to the Italian customs official who, having cursorily examined his passport, waved him on over the border. He accelerated away into Italy, down several hundreds of miles of autostrada constructed to convey vehicles towards the Appennines at the fastest, if not the safest, speed.

'Goodbye, le and la. Farewell, un and une. Now we are in sunny Italia away from all that old ordure. Boys! Here-a is-a the land-a where every butcher's lad sings Verdi. Una voce poca fa!' he warbled in high tenor.

'That's Rossini, darling. And it's a soprano aria.'

'No matter, it's the spirit that matters. Il spirito. Che gelida manina,' he screeched.

'And now you're into Puccini.'

'Votre petit main est glacé,' Bernard sang on, unperturbed, 'Alors! Je me chaud it into vie . . .' He reverted to the spoken word. 'Entering l'Italia always make-a me feel free. Li-*bro*! Make-a me want to celebrate the avventura of being alive. I feel so at home.'

They sped through tunnel after tunnel, and were advised to switch on their lanterns, over bridges and viaducts, warned all the while of dangerous cross winds. At every kilometre of the way there were instructions of how they should behave on this marvel of modern engineering. Bernard mostly obeyed them, which was more than could be said for some of the natives who seemed intent on reaching Mary's bosom rather more swiftly than the Virgin herself had been officially decreed to have ascended. He remained, nonetheless, elated. 'L'Italia! Je t'adore, je t'adore!'

Penny attempted to interest the boys in a new game. 'You count the number of tunnels. And you count the bridges. And you count in Italian, Simon, and you in French, Brian.'

'That's not fair. I don't know Italian.'

'We'll do it together. This one is otto . . . because I've been counting secretly all the time . . . so the next is?'

'Neuf.'

'You're counting bridges, Brian.'

'Well, I've counted five and they've *sank*. And I wish Dad wouldn't drive so fast. *Sank*, do you get it, Bob?'

'I'm not into a counting situation. I'm just keeping my eyes shut and pretending we're descending into Dante's Inferno.'

'Is that where we're staying?'

'Most likely.'

They zoomed on for another hundred miles or so, Bernard commenting ecstatically on the technical skill which had made the road possible. 'You don't wonder these people have come down from the Romans! I mean, just think of visualizing anything like this. Cutting through these mountains. *And* they're bankrupt. In absoluta liquidazzione.'

'Isn't it time we stopped for coffee?'

'Servizio!' roared Bernard in bass. 'Serviziani!' In tenor.

He swung the car into a lay-by. 'Ici, signora, signore, la trattoria autostrada, pronto.'

'Prego,' said Bob, adding, 'that's what they always say. Don't mean a thing kids. Just a friendly neighbourhood greeting.'

'Prego,' repeated Brian and Simon in unison, and experimented maddeningly with the word in several keys and with much crescendo until an elderly tramp approached the car and made obsequious appeals for money. Bernard said, 'Bella! Bella!' indicating the bright azure sky, and the man looked mystified. 'Per favore,' he requested, bowing low. Bob handed him a note and the poor wretch indicated

98

his willingness to wash the windscreen but none of them understood, so they all said 'Prego' several times and the tramp attended to the next car, feeling he had done his best.

In the motorway restaurant organization had run riot, directing customers through crash barriers and along a maze of metal-framed passageways at the end of which was a free area where the eating house became a supermarket selling everything from food and drink to enormous plastic dolls wrapped in polythene. The Plums made their purchases and queued in another aluminium passage to pay for them. Bernard presented a 50,000 lire note which led to agitated comment from the cashier who thumped several knobs on her register, handed Bernard a pile of greasy notes, and caused a cascade of individually wrapped bonbons to descend a chute designed for small coins. There was a shortage of currency, she explained.

'La bata! Bene. Bene. Graartzieh, signorina.' The cashier smiled uncomprehendingly. 'Prego,' she said, automatically.

'Hope they're not like those rotten French sweets,' said Brian.

Bernard silenced his son by yelling 'Graartzieh' several times, and then applied himself to forcing his party through several more crash barriers and back to the car where the tramp was applying a dirty rag to the windscreen.

'Graartzieh!' Bernard handed him a fistful of bonbons which were accepted sullenly.

As they sat on the tailboard of the car having their elevenses in the sunshine Bob enquired, 'So where we makin' for, huh?'

'Until this moment I don't even know myself.' Bernard took a sealed envelope marked *One* from his wallet. 'This whole trip is top security.'

'Why?' Penny felt impatient, irritated. 'It's only a feature in a fairly second-rate rag.'

'Which is paying me handsomely. So we accept their conditions. Il conditioni, to put it in the vernacular.'

'No need. We all speak English.'

'And you know what happened up there in Frogland with Trafford and Annabelle doublecrossing us? It may all seem a bit silly but it's our pane e margarino . . .'

'Burro, burro!'

'Keep your cool, Pen. The project is different this time. We are to visit seven places which I have to describe in an obfuscating way . . .'

'Just use your Francitaliano.'

'. . .In an obfuscating way. And the readers have to fit the place to the description, the right hotel to the right place. Then they win a major prize, like a spin-drier or a week in sunny Italia for two.'

'With you in the background singing che gelida manina, I get it. A real holiday situation.'

'So where are we going tonight?' demanded Penny.

'To one of the most romantic places in the whole of Italy. You'd jump for joy if I told you.'

'Well . . . *where*?'

'Mustn't say till we get there.'

'Don't be so childish.'

'Them's me instructions.'

'Does it begin with an R?' enquired Brian.

'It is not Reggio.'

'With an S?'

'It is not Santa Margherita, Simon!'

'P?' Penny joined in.

'I'm not saying.'

'It obviously does then.'

'I shan't answer another question.'

'Italian town beginning with P? One of the most romantic places in the whole country. Piacenza . . . no. Parma . . . no-o. Must be Pisa.' Bernard sulked and put up the bonnet of the car pretending to check oil and batteries.

The exit to Pisa was signposted and the boys were soon excitedly looking for the leaning tower. 'Last one to see it's a cissy,' yelled Brian.

'I should warn you,' said Bernard, clearing his throat a few times and tugging at his beard to indicate that something not altogether pleasing was coming. 'I should warn you that Donald will be rejoining us shortly.'

'Oh no!' cried the boys in unison.

'Why?' asked their mother.

'Did I ever tell you about Fauna and the Inconcubine, as she called it. Incunabula to you. Meaning, boys, books printed before 1500.'

'Groan, groan,' said Simon.

'Donald, as you may know, is an authority on incunabula. And it seems that much attention is being given to two missing items which are somewhere in this actual Italia. They are especially valuable because although they are printed, they are also interleaved with illuminated manuscripts.'

'Dazzle, dazzle!'

'And the Russians want to get hold of them. Some batty woman called Freda Mock-Templeton has written a learned paper suggesting that the original illuminations were done

101

for Tamburlaine the Great, who was not actually the tyrant we've always supposed him to be but the first great communist leader.'

'Or the tyrant we always supposed him to be.'

'Please yourself, Bob. Anyhow, the Russians are dead keen to get these books, which are missals, and house them in a museum in Moscow. Their agents are trying to track them down.'

'Snoop, snoop.'

'In addition, it appears that friend Proggle, who was recently converted to Rome, has also dedicated himself to finding them. It's his crusade. So the other press barons, naturally, are trying to find them first. But we're working with the expert – namely Donald. I wonder if Fauna's still doing Proggle's detective work and, if so, with whom?'

'Prise, prise.'

Bob, not too gently, knocked the twins' heads together, at which, undismayed, they cried in unison, 'Crunch, crunch.'

They arrived at Pisa and unloaded at a hotel close to the cathedral complex.

A suite of rooms had been booked for them which, curiously, was entered by a door at the back of the hotel office, immediately beside a high-speed typist who inclined her head and flashed a smile of welcome at them as she tapped away industriously at her qwertyuiop.

In the first room was a double bed on which Penny and Bernard dumped their suitcases. In the next were two singles, obviously intended for the boys, and, in the last, another single, which Bob, with misgivings, agreed to occupy, realizing that his only means of exit were either through the window into an inner courtyard where a lone cypress mournfully grew, or back through the Plums' rooms. There was neither private bathroom nor loo. He felt trapped, and his tummy rumbled warningly.

Bernard pulled back the shutters in the double room and noted that the view was mostly of the tower, which leaned in the direction of the hotel. 'I think,' he said to Penny, 'we should push the bed over that side.'

'Whatever for?'

'So that the tower misses us. If it falls, you see? The boys'll be all right. Their room is definitely off course. Unless the whole hotel caves in under the impact.'

Seated on the forecourt of the hotel, sipping a campari-soda, and thinking to himself, if I had a bad cold I could be persuaded that germs might flee before such a filthy taste yet I'm supposed to be drinking this for enjoyment, Bernard heard a familiar voice saying, 'Helloo, darl, so pleased to find you alone.'

Fauna Wynyates slid into the chair beside him. 'I have to talk to you most urgently. Can we be overheard?'

'There may be someone lurking behind the arras . . .'

'Don't make fun. I'll speak in a low voice. Listen, you know about the missals . . .'

'I know what a missal is.'

'Don't give anything away, darl. What you don't know is that someone else is after them.'

'But I do. The Russians.'

'Not only. The Arabs want them too.'

'I've heard rumours of conversion in high places but that's absurd.'

'They've become terribly acquisitive. They want to buy up everything of value against the time when the oil runs dry.'

Bernard remained sceptically silent.

'They tried to squeeze me off the road on the autostrada. I all but went into the ditch. They'll do it to you, darl. We're being watched all the time.' She got closer and Bernard didn't enjoy the intimacy. Supposing Penny should come out?

'This is what you have to do, darl . . .'

'Fauna, I haven't met these Arabs yet. What do they look like?'

'Real Arabs, darl. In burnouses, like Lawrence. Now, you must let them know you know where the missals are, then they won't liquidate you. They'll follow you to the place instead.'

'And liquidate me there. No matter. I don't know where they are.'

Bernard rose and walked about the hotel forecourt, returning to stand by Fauna's chair, 'You were going to follow the Ay-rabs and trick us all, letting Proggle win the booty. Miss Wynyates, dear, you're playing it dirty. Bye now. Love to Arthur.'

Bernard went quickly to his room muttering, 'How devious can you get? How deviato? Deviatino . . . deviatissimo . . .'

'Do you need a dictionary or something?' Penny asked.

'I may need a bodyguard . . .'

Bernard continued to brood about Fauna and the likelihood or otherwise of the Arab agents being in the hotel. He was seated waiting for dinner, again on the forecourt of the hotel, but now with his family around him. They sat facing the cathedral complex.

'It moved!'

'What did, Bernie?'

'The tower.'

'Don't be ridiculous.'

'I tell you it moved. I saw it. There it goes again!'

'Sit down, darling. You're making an ass of yourself.'

'I'd rather be an ass than an ostrich.'

'It only moves,' Brian observed, ponderously, 'one eighth of a millimetre every year. I don't think you'd see that, Dad.'

'In any case, Bernie, the thing's been in a standing situation eight hundred years or so. You got an awful good chance of not being here when it does topple.'

'On the contrary, from the viewpoint of mathematical probability, the fact that it has *not* toppled during eight hundred years must mean the actual moment of disaster is closer.'

'Bernard,' said Penny, 'it might occur to you that this is all rather silly talk . . .' She indicated the boys.

'I'm not scared.'

'Not afraid of an old tower.'

'There you are! Not frightened, nor am I. I'm just being realistic.'

'Buona sera, signora, signori.' A dark-haired waiter greeted them, all flashing white teeth and menus.

'Sera! Sera! A che s'appelez-vous camera-airy?'

'What are you trying to say, Bernard?'

'I want to know his name.'

'I am Umberto, signore.'

'What's fagiolini?' asked Simon, studying the menu.

'Beans.'

'Like Heinz?'

'Not like Heinz,' replied Penny.

'I'd like fagiolini. Sounds good.'

They all fell to repeating names on the menu because they liked the sounds they thought they represented. Umberto stood patiently, smiling engagingly.

Bernard said they should all have pasta dishes because this was pasta country, but Penny demurred on the grounds that it was fattening. 'Veal escalope is equally traditional.'

'But, Mum, we don't eat veal because of factory farming.'

'Different, Simon, here,' said his father. 'They have free range veals. I saw them grazing all the way down the autostrada.' So the boys chose spaghetti because they foresaw comic possibilities in eating it. Bob adventurously chose Bomba di Riso to find out what it was, Penny and Bernard settled for veal, and the latter insisted they must have salad.

'Due insalata di tomato.'

'Signore?'

'Per favore. What have I said wrong?'

'I guess tomato is just not an Italian word.'

'Not an Italian word? Tomato? You could scarcely get more so.'

'Nevertheless, try pommodoro. You may get what you want.'

'Insalata pommodoro,' said Umberto, rapidly. 'Due?'

'Oui. Yes. Si. My God, it's confusing being multilingual. Now what about vino plonko?'

'Si, signore.'

'Alora! Not to mention prego. Vino rouge-o. Non. Vino rosso. E *secco*. Comprenez-vous?'

106

'You like red wine, sir? Chianti?'

'Non fizzante. Molto pas de fizzy.'

'Don't they have a carafe wine?'

'That won't stop it being fizzante. But a good idea. What's Italiano for vin du pays?'

'You like local wine, signore? Verra good.'

'Bene, bene. Una caraffa, peuta-tettra . . .'

Umberto looked willing but perplexed so Bernard attempted to clarify their needs. 'Scusi, per favore, una caraffa vino reddo.'

'Si, signore.'

'E non fizzante.'

'Si. We 'ave very good aste spumante. Better than champagne.'

'No. Non. *Nona.* Umberto – Umberti – Umbertissimo. I *do not want it fiz* – fizzy – *fizzante*. Still. *Still*? I want.'

'Steel, signore?'

'Si. Come acqua potabile.'

'Si.'

'And aussi. What's also? Can't think . . . Alora. Alora in additione, vino blanco, molto secco, and molto caldo . . .'

'No dear friend,' amended Bob, quickly. 'Caldo is hot. You mean fredo.'

'*Frey*-do,' corrected Bernard. 'You pronounce "e" as "ay".'

'But you don't want it caldo, all the same.'

'I don't indeed. Thanks, Bob. Absurd language. Imagine "caldo" meaning the opposite of what it says.'

Umberto patiently studied his order pad. 'So, signore, one caraffa red wine, one caraffa white wine, secco.'

'E due,' said Penny, 'coca cola, per favore.'

'Pas de still,' added Simon, but Umberto had sped away.

'It would be simpler if we all spoke English,' suggested

107

Penny but as Umberto served the first course Bernard again felt the urge to communicate in what he thought of as the local lingo. 'Io non voglio,' he began, pointing at the tower, 'il toro to cadere.'

Umberto, understanding not a word, replied, soothingly, 'Si.'

'Molto incidente si il cadere.' Bernard couldn't leave it alone.

Umberto, to change the subject, whilst automatically ogling Penny who had come within range of vision, commented, 'Two years I was in London.'

'In Soho?'

'Friss Street, signora. I enjoy verra much but not like the wessa. My wife-a not like it either. We come home. Pisa. Is nice place. You like it?'

'Molto much.'

'Business is-a good. Many visitors.'

'Mind you, Umberto, if the old toro did topple – cadere – that would put paid to tourism, yes?'

'Grazie, signore.' Umberto sped away. There was a limit to the time he could afford to spend on this lunatic Englishman.

After dinner Bernard and Bob crossed the grass to the baptistery around which they strolled, much affected by the tranquillity and balminess of the evening until, coming again in sight of the cathedral, two Arabs wearing burnouses came towards them.

'My God, she was right,' Bernard gasped. 'Down!'

He fell flat on the grass.

Bob looked down at him in astonishment.

'Down, down! They may be dangerous. Pericoloso!'

The Arabs passed out of sight and Bernard rose, dusting his trousers, saying, 'That was close. Better get back.'

Bob said gently, 'Now I'll help you past the tower, Bernie. Don't look up.'

As he climbed into bed Bernard said 'I've seen the Arabs. We really are being followed.'

'That's right,' murmured Penny, sleepily. 'Have a different obsession. It'll make the blood rush to another part of your brain.'

Bernard snorted and said he hoped they wouldn't have to stay long in Pisa. He tried to sleep. Presently there was a knock at the door and Bob said, 'Excuse me. The john.' He disappeared through the other door to the office, from whence still came the clack of incessant typing.

'What a fantastic arrangement!'

'Think beautiful thoughts,' advised Penny. 'Lie very still.'

'I'd rather perform beautiful actions.'

'No,' she said, rejecting his embrace. 'Not on a public right of way.'

Penny dozed off, and Bob lumbered through apologizing profusely.

Bernard slept fitfully and was having a dream about Fauna, with oil gushing from her ears, being pursued by two villainous Arab horsemen, when he was awakened by an urgent rapping. 'Terribly sorry, folks. But I gotta bother you again.'

Preposterous, thought Bernard, irritated all the more because Penny was obviously deeply asleep, breathing heavily. Bob crept back, hitting several creaking floorboards and muttering, 'Christ, I'm sorry, I truly am sorry.' Meanwhile the typist went on bashing her machine at sound-breaking speed.

Bernard was having a nightmare about the tower. He woke up to a thundering on the door from the office and a female voice screaming, 'Signore Ploom! Signore Ploom!'

'Penny, quick, quick! Boys! It's falling. We must get out.'
Bernard leapt from the bed in terror. The beating on the
door continued. Penny woke, startled.

'*Signore Ploom!*' Bernard rushed to the door and the
typist said, 'For you, signore. Telefono.'

'What about the tower?'

The typist said, 'Telefono. Lon-don.'

Bernard, dishevelled, almost indecent in loose pyjamas,
grabbed the phone. 'Plum,' said a voice, abruptly. '*Gazette*.
Listen. Gideon Apthorpe-Harebrook here. We want you to
get off to San Gimignano first thing in the morning.'

'Delighted. Can't tell you how disturbed I've been by this
wretched tower here . . .'

'Go to the Albergo Domodossola, right? There's a woman
there called Freda Mock-Templeton . . .'

'I heard of her. The lady the Russians . . .'

'Right.' Gideon's imperious tone derived from his years of
fame as a television interviewer, a position he had lost when
there was a change of power at high level. 'Now don't tell her
who you are, son, but get friendly. She may give you a clue
on the missals. Otherwise, we have to rely on your Uncle
Donald, whom you pick up in Siena, day after tomorrow,
yes?'

'As you say.'

'And go on sending in copy about the hotels. Series is still
hot. But watch out for a wicked bitch called Fauna, son.'

'I know her.'

'Keep clear. She's working for the Arabs.'

Bernard returned to his room and, while Penny slept and
Bob passed through at intervals, he wrote his copy in biro.
Then, when he realized no one, least of all himself, could
read his handwriting, he moved into the office whilst he
could still remember what he had written, and typed out his

message on the machine which the hotel typist had at last vacated.

He had just finished when a middle-aged man in singlet, trousers and vast paunch, with braces hanging at his ample sides, burst in and said, in booming tones, '*No*! *No*! *Signore*! You must not use. This is hotel ossif. You disturba guests who sleep. Is verra late.'

'My wife is fast asleep. Actually, she is a topo dormitorio, comprendere-airy-airy-airy? Anyway, finito. Scusi. Buona notte.'

'Pardon me,' said Bob, entering the office yet again. 'Guess I should've booked a john with a bed.'

Bernard emerged from the Plum suite into the light of the office where the typist was already fingering away, and made for the open-air part of the restaurant where he sank into a chair.

'Camer-air-er-ree!' He shouted, half-heartedly. 'Per favore, breakfastina.'

Umberto hove into view.

'You like egg, sair?'

'No, just cappucino, per vous plait.'

Umberto looked crestfallen. 'I think Inglese like egg for breakfast.'

'Graatzieh,' mumbled Bernard, no fight left in him.

Umberto proudly returned shortly with a boiled egg which he placed in a glass that instantly cracked, making a pinging sound on the quiet morning air which set Bernard's shattered nerves a-jangle again.

111

Moderately restored by two large coffees, and joined by Penny, he set out to look for a bank. They entered a branch of the Banco Santa Spirito and joined a queue at the only part of the counter which was operative, noting that in shortage of manpower Italian banks in no way differed from those in Britain.

A voluble argument was going on between a man with a fistful of documents and a polite but implacable clerk. Mostly they talked at the same time and it sounded as though artoro-benedetti-michel-angeli-spaghetti-bolognese was being repeated over and over again, punctuated by any number of prontos and pregos.

In due course the documents-man sighed and retired to a table where he puzzled over the forms exclaiming unceasingly, 'ravioli incastrati'.

Soon it was Bernard's turn. He smiled ingratiatingly and waved his passport. 'Shraveller sheck. Cam-bi-o. Per favore?'

'You are at the wrong counter, signore. Over there, please.'

Penny said, 'Just speak English, for God's sake. You embarrass me.' She left Bernard and sat at the other end of the banking hall.

A beautifully dressed young man, attired in the height of fashion, and admiring himself in the polished top of the counter, deigned to look up after a few moments.

'What is ess-shange rate?'

'Quattromilletrentocinque.'

'Scusi?'

'Quattromilletrentocinque, signore. I write it down.'

'Sank you. 1435! Piccolo amounto, pronto, signore?'

'Over there,' said the clerk, returning to his narcissism and indicating a barred cash desk where Bernard was handed several bank notes in huge denominations, and a pile of small coins.

'Pas de caramellay, signore?'

'Signore?'

'In autostrada magazino . . . Supermarketto, si?'

'Si, signore, next door. Is called Centra.'

'Nonno, nonno.' Bernard produced a sweet from his pocket and passed it across the counter. 'Autostrada caramellay.'

The clerk accepted it graciously and turned to a newspaper. On the front page were large photos of Proggle and Avonbury and a headline – 'SCANDALO DELLA MONTAGNA DI FORMAGGIO.

Seeing Bernard's interest the clerk remarked, 'Your English lord make a profit from E.E.C. Not good, signore.'

'I'm sorry.' Bernard assumed national proportions of guilt. 'What he do?'

'He tells Brussels he buy surplus cheese. He pay for it. Then he try sell it to Rhodesians but not allowed. Then he try Russians and they say, yes. But he sell to Chinese although Russians say they pay more. Very funny, yes?'

'So?'

'Russians angry. Brussels angry. British government very angry. Everyone angry.'

'Rotten old Proggers. I once work for him.'

The Italian was not interested. 'Also,' he said.

'Si?'

'In Italy we very angry.'

'Pour questa?'

'Cheese is Bel Paese.'

113

As they left the bank Bernard complained that the Holy Spirit gave a very poor rate of exchange.

'Signora? Buon'giorno!'

'It's Dino.'

Bernard noticed a handsome Italian waving at his wife from across the street, teeth flashing, eyes sparkling, black hair gleaming.

'Who's that?'

'That is Leonardo Giovanni Dino-dino Caradente-Vecchio.'

'It's worse than Artoro Benedetti Michelangeli.'

'Dino for short. I met him in the Massif when you were at Cagnes.'

'You didn't mention him.'

No, reflected Penny, as Dino dextrously swerved across the busy street as though dancing a tango with the traffic, she hadn't.

'Dino, this is my husband, Bernard Plum. Bernie, Dino.'

'So, you are here on a story, Signore Plum?'

'Not really. A series of articles.'

'And you work for this Lord Proggle?'

'No longer.'

'Sit down. Have a coffee? Glass of vino? Cameriere!'

They took a table at a kerbside café. 'I am on holiday, see. My home here in Pisa. But my paper call me to work on this scandalo del'formaggio. You hear about it, this cheese mountain? It make me very upset. Is very wrong to treat Italian cheese like this. Cheese very expensive here in Italy. I think common market is good for French, not for us.'

'All we get out of it, Dino, is French rotten apples. Delicioso d'Oro, as you say.'

'Tell about this Proggle.'

Bernard recalled a conversation at the Hotel Terrasse

Ombragée.

He excused himself and ran back to the hotel where he called Gideon Apthorpe-Harebrook.

'Listen, this cheese mountain scandal?'

'What about it?'

'In my view it may be significant that about a week ago when Proggle of the *Sabbatical* gave a dinner party at Draguignan, France, Lord Ted Fountainshorn, chairman of the National Cheese Board, was present.'

'He's already resigned. Don't you read the papers?'

Dejected, Bernard returned to the café where he didn't at all like the way Dino appeared to be flirting with Penny. Even less did he like the way she was flirting with him.

'What I don't understand is, why has he sold it to the Chinese? They don't eat cheese, do they?'

'It was the idea of this English lord. He thought, times are changing in China. New thinking. New traditions. He will sell them cheese. Part of cultural revolution. You know what I think?'

Penny, reading Bernard's thoughts accurately – if not Dino's – decided to be tactful, and, having already got out her lipstick, said, in the act of applying it, 'Ot oo hink?'

Bernard got in first. 'It wouldn't surprise me if those inscrutable Chinks weren't going to sell it to someone else at a profit.'

Bob was much recovered by the time they set off for the ring road around Pisa. He sang cowboy hill-billies which delighted the boys but irritated Bernard.

'What I'd appreciate now,' pleaded the driver, looking in his mirror and seeing an Arab in a burnous at the wheel of a yellow Fiat right behind him, 'would be someone telling me which direction to Florence, spelt in these heathen parts, F-I-R-E-N-Z-E.'

'You just missed the turning.'

'This ring road is making me giddy.' He glanced frequently in his driving mirror as he circulated the city again. The yellow Fiat was trailing him. He slowed down; it slowed down. He signalled to turn into a lay-by; it did the same but, at the moment when it should have completed the manoeuvre, its trafficator was cancelled and it went on, to the consternation of a trailing coach which honked and swerved. Bernard sat in the lay-by and said, 'Serve him right.' Then a second yellow Fiat sped past, also driven by an Arab, although a lady sat at his side. Bernard set off again and, at the appropriate place, turned in the direction of Firenze, noting that, at the first lay-by, a yellow Fiat was stationary. Where was the other?

He sped on down the autostrada to Florence and it seemed to him that many small yellow Fiats passed him the other side of the motorway intersection – as indeed they did – and in each one he thought he detected an Arab seated beside Fauna. He became confused and when he saw a sign to Siena he followed it, hoping to escape all other traffic. Having got some way down a minor road he stopped to consult a map. 'Every sign points to Livorno. Whatever does that mean?'

'I guess we call it Leghorn.'

'That doesn't help. What do you mean, "Leghorn"? Liv doesn't mean leg, does it?'

'No,' said Simon, 'but "orno" could mean "horn".'

'Shut up, Simon,' they all chorused.

116

They motored on and entered a hamlet named Vinci.

'This on your route, Caesar?'

'Something's wrong.'

'Don't those two little yellow Fiats look sweet?' remarked Penny. 'Parked on that rubbish dump.'

Bernard put his foot down and left Vinci in a cloud of dust, driving with reckless abandon until a major road was signed to the Autostrada and the South.

'Must get away from those damned Fiats.'

Immediately one sped into view approaching him at 70 miles an hour.

'Which of them was it?'

'Whichever of them has become a mother superior. And do take care, darling.'

They milled about the Tuscan countryside for nearly two hours, the winding, undulating roads cutting their speed. At last there was a sign to Poggibonsi which Simon noticed just in time to prevent his father turning left for Siena. Grunted gratitude was his reward until Bernard recovered his temper announcing, 'I have always thought that this Tuscany . . .' (he manouvred round several hairpin bends expertly)' . . . is one of the world's ideal regions. Somewhere I could really settle.'

'You probably will, if you don't take the next bend more carefully. Bernard, *mind*!'

An enormous furniture lorry hurled itself towards them on the wrong side, hooting wildly, and Bernard flung his car into a hedgerow. 'That was a bit close,' he murmured, revving hard to extricate his vehicle from a ditch.

'Be more careful then.'

'*Me* be more careful!'

They reached Poggibonsi and, to their relief, saw San Gimignano signed down a road across which was an unguarded railway crossing. At the very moment that Bernard was shouting gleefully. 'Santa Jim, here we come,' there was a shrill toot which made him look about but he could see nothing in his mirror or on the approach road to cause alarm. He changed down to go over the rails and there was an urgent ferocious trumpeting. He again flung his car sideways, and into a ditch, as a single carriage locomotive trundled across the roadway.

They sat there, bemused, astonished to be alive. Gradually they became indignant. A small crowd gathered and spoke volubly, at great length. Then, as the moment of hysteria was reached, the crowd suddenly grew calm and threw itself on Bernard's car, wrenching it from the ditch. 'Grazies' filled the air, there was much laughter and congratulation. Bernard offered sheaves of bank notes which were refused, although several people rushed upon him to shake his hand. He started the engine and drove off across the level crossing just as another train whistle rent the air.

'Of all the ridiculous places! You'd think they'd put up a sign. Don't they want custom? And the road surface looks as though it hasn't been repaired since the last of the legions marched away.'

'I think the entrance was back there,' ventured Penny, 'by the workman's hut. There was a turning . . .'

'But that's an old cart track . . .'

'It wouldn't be the first time.'

Brian said, 'There's a sign on a tree up there.'

'It's no use telling them,' his brother commented, bitterly. 'They won't take any notice. I saw that sign years ago.'

'Shut up, Simon.'

'There you are!' Simon punched Brian to relieve his feelings.

'He's quite right,' said Penny. 'Thank you, Brian. The sign is so overgrown by weeds!'

'Typical,' said Bernard and began to turn his vehicle, which provoked a clamour of honking and flashing as an Alfa Romeo flew by throwing up hundreds of flints which rapped against the bodywork and windscreen of Bernard's already abroad-scarred car. He honked and flashed back, yelling, 'Lu-*nat*-ico! Lento, Lento! Andantino! Molto lento! Their windscreens must be made of tungsten.'

They proceeded down a narrow drive, shrouded in trees and shrubs.

'I bet that dreadful Trafford's waiting at the next bend to ambush us.'

But round the corner the trees gave way to a wide meadow at the end of which stood a sprawling villa with its stuccoed walls peeling badly – The Albergo Domodossola.

'Watch out for wolves,' warned Brian.

As they left the car a youth came through the open front door and bade them welcome.

'I believe someone may actually be going to carry our bagagio. Buon'giorno, Chico! Il patrone, per favore? Indiso, si?'

'Yes sir. Good afternoon, madam. Please go into reception.'

'You English?'

'Very cosmopolitan staff here. All races. Even some Eyeties. If you unlock the tailgate, I'll get your luggage.'

At the reception desk a large middle-aged woman with liquid eyes and seraphic expression greeted Bernard warmly and suggested the family take tea on the terrace. 'You are tired from your journey. Billy will take up your cases.' She spoke with a slight Italian accent, and then broke off to address a girl at the desk beside her in rapid French. 'Excuse me,' she smiled. 'Many things to remember,' a remark amplified by a sudden torrent of German directed at two podgy, elderly women whom she saw about to leave the hotel, and for whom she had mail.

The terrace, on several levels, overlooked an olive grove. Guests basked in the afternoon sunshine and there was only one unoccupied table, one tier down, at the end of an overhanging stone balcony next to an L-shaped bench on which sat three persons of distinct poise and self-possession, two of them smoking cigarettes through yard-long holders.

'I told Gombrich it was a Lotto,' said one of the women. 'I had only to glance at it. Who else would have placed an angel at that angle? K. Clark may talk till he's ultramarine in the face to convince me it's a Lippi, but I know my Lotto.'

'There's a madonna,' the other woman said quickly as her friend stopped to draw breath, 'in the church of Santa Maria della Pineta at Tuberovescusa, about which I used to have such tussles with B. Berenson. He insisted it was a Giotto, if you please. A Giotto, I ask you!' Her voice dropped several registers. 'I'd like to know,' she added darkly, 'when Giotto ever went to Tuberovescusa.' She also *laughed* darkly.

Both ladies were in their forties and had finely chiselled features incorporating thinly pencilled-in eyebrows. Their hairstyles were similar, fringed, unwaved and short, and they wore simple, sleeveless dresses in bright colours.

'Can't tell you how angry I was this afternoon,' said the man in the group, almost allowing the woman's laugh to die away. 'They'd run out of slides at San Domenico in Siena. You know San Domenico don't you, where Saint Kate had her trances?'

'Saint Kate, he calls her.' The women laughed affectedly. 'Rodge, really!'

'You know who I mean. She's just like a gargoyle on York Minster; t'one I've always called Margaret Thatcher.' He spoke in an assumed north country accent but it was known that he was the son of a duke, and legitimate at that. His age was totally disguised by a huge mop of black hair, an unruly beard covering most of his face, and tiny, tinted, oval spectacles with silver frames. He wore a cream tee-shirt with mystic initials and a pair of flared blue jeans. He was a painter who specialized in doors; what Andy Warhol was to canned beans, Rodge Barnsley was to hardboard doors. He was without peer. 'Anyways,' he went on, 'there's a Matteo di Giovanni there that I've been trying to get a slide of for years. It's very upsetting, I don't mind telling you. T'country 'ere is not what it were in Vasari's time.'

'Vasari's time,' shrieked one woman. 'Rodge, be serious! Gemma will show you up in her frightful magazine if you say these awful things.'

At which point their attention was momentarily diverted towards the Plum group as tea was served, and they had to draw in their cigarette holders to allow the waiter to pass by. The woman who wasn't Gemma bowed elegantly to Bernard as she caught his eye and said, 'Isn't it a captivating view? So quintessentially Tuscan. And when did you ever see a more Tiepolan sky?'

'Perfect,' admitted Bernard. 'It reminds me of the background to so many Renaissance canvasses. You know? When you look past all the religiosity in the foreground and there, behind the haloes, is the incomparable Tuscan countryside. Marvellous!'

The ladies looked astounded and Bob added, slyly, 'I

guess I'm more into the Eye-talian Ren-ay-sence than my friend here. We really came on account of my needing to see the Ghirlandaios.'

'Really?' Gemma drew on her cigarette, holding the pause so long as she dared. 'One doesn't really come to San Gimignano for what it has to offer in the way of great art. It's just blessedly quiet after the uproar of Siena and Firenze.'

'Yes, it's so peaceful and tranquil here. That olive grove,' Penny said feelingly, thinking it time she contributed and, anyhow, these women's voices were spoiling it all. Immediately she wished she hadn't because they looked at her intently – even Rodge looked at her intently from behind his little, oval, tinted lenses – all three making mental notes about which artist her profile reminded them. Penny felt two inches tall and added, lamely, 'This sort of thing appeals to me. Nature.'

She was saved further embarrassment by the arrival of an Arab who appeared dramatically on the balcony above them and looked, with slit eyes, and tight mouth, above which a thin, thirties-style moustache grew, quickly around him. His eyes stayed on their group for a moment, then he turned, made a miniscule twitch of his right cheek to some unseen companion, and disappeared.

'My God,' said Gemma, 'don't say the signora is selling out to the Ay-rabs. It's frightful at home now; they're buying everything.'

'Nay,' said Rodge, drily, 'I 'eard they'd made a bid for Offa's Dyke, Freda?'

'Did you address your friend as Freda?'

'That's her name.'

'You wouldn't be,' said Bernard, with sickening humility, 'Dr Freda Mock-Templeton, lecturer in Florentine Painting at the Offa's Dyke College of Art? Who wrote that extraordinarily interesting paper on Tamerlane being the first true Communist would you?'

Freda laughed almost up a whole scale, very flattered. 'I was really only flying a kite.'

Bernard looked disappointed. 'I thought you meant it.'

Freda laughed almost down a whole scale. 'Don't tell me you are another Russian agent?'

'Have they been getting at you, then?'

'They have. Isn't that so, Gemma?'

'I told Freda she should accept their filthy lucre. After all, what's an old missal? Anyhow, Freda's been jumped over by too many men.' She spat out the last word and Rodge grinned. 'She ought by rights to have the National by now, or the Tate.'

'I don't understand,' Bernard said (overdoing the stupid act, Penny thought). 'What's this about a missal?'

Freda explained, very patronizingly. Gemma, who turned out to be gallery correspondent of *Life Class* joined in. 'Of course, you know, after the invention of printing there were many aristos who felt it was très chic to go on having illuminated manuscripts. Printing, to them, was vulgar. And there were others who compromised, and interleaved their printed books with handwork. It wasn't common, there are very few examples left. . .'

'So, where are these missals then?'

Freda laughed both up and down the whole scale. 'Well, you may ask! That's what all the furore is about. What the Russians want to know.'

'Why's that? Guess I didn't know the Russians were into a missal situation.'

'They think, foolish people, that Tamerlane's descendants owned one or both missals,' Freda explained and Gemma added, 'They choose to think that because they want some more loot in their museums. I don't think they actually believe it . . .'

'I begin to wish I'd never written that article. I was really only repeating a bit of old folk gossip.'

Two Arabs now appeared on the balcony pretending to admire the view but frequently looking in Freda's direction. Gemma noticed them. 'Looks to me as though the Ay-rabs want them also. They are certainly very taken with you, Freda.'

'Don't be disgusting,' she said, shuddering. 'They have female company already.' Fauna Wynyates had joined them.

'So,' Bernard doggedly pursued the subject. 'There are absolutely no clues as to where these missals might be?'

'It is thought,' said Freda, 'that one of them is kept hidden in a church in Frascati, and there is a legend that its twin is somewhere on an island in a lake. There are a great many lakes in Italy and exploring them is going to take rather a long while. There is just a hope, if we can see the one in Frascati, that it might give some clue as to the exact whereabouts of its twin. The problem is that the custodian of the one in Frascati refuses to show it to anyone.'

Bernard felt he had grilled her sufficiently. 'Well, how very interesting. I must wish you a successful outcome, Doctor.'

The Arabs and Fauna turned abruptly and left the balcony as the Plum family rose to go to their rooms, leaving Bob with their new acquaintances.

Bernard was relieved to see Fauna and the Arabs driving off. The signora beckoned him and said, 'The English lady left you a letter.' Fauna had scribbled very briefly on a piece of hotel notepaper. 'I'm only *pretending* to play along with the two sheikhs. Are *they* furious about the price they pay for petrol here!'

Which gave Bernard something to ponder about as he returned to the top balcony where he heard Rodge saying to Bob, in a rebuking voice, 'when it comes to Lippi it's always crucial, I think, to ensure not confusing Filippino with Filippo.'

'Absolutely,' confirmed Freda and Gemma, nodding agreement.

'I guess I like the one who painted those – er – round pictures,' said Bob, deadpan. 'I'm really into painting in the round.'

They stared at him inscrutably for a moment, each privately deciding he resembled a Francis Bacon.

Tina and Adrian Longhorn had flown into Pisa that day, hired a car and come on to the Domodossola at which they had stayed countless times previously. Adrian had made many notes on the plane and needed only to refresh his memory briefly before phoning through his copy to the *Wanderer*, which was promising its readers holidays in Italy as prizes for working out the hidden clues in the new series. He was aware that Fauna was working on the missal angle but had had difficulty in contacting her, which was a pity, he felt, because the paper was hinting darkly that Lord Proggle was about to make an amazing discovery of interest to antiquarians. He thought he should have been told more but supposed that was the way newspapermen were treated. More worrying were the stories carried in rival publications suggesting that Proggle and his associates had cheated the

E.E.C. out of several million lire.

However, Adrian was enjoying his free holiday, having resigned from Ware, and being on the lookout for a likely property to purchase in Italy. He exalted in the luxury of being at the Domodossola again, and sat on the terrace, drinking in the view. Bernard sat down at the adjoining table. Adrian greeted him proprietorially, 'Been here before?'

'No, first time.'

'You'll come again. This must be our sixth, no – seventh visit. Really is perfect. Though I'm not used to having to *work* when I'm here.'

He wants to tell me his life story, thought Bernard.

'Yes, I've a little *chore* to do to keep my wits flexed.'

He's *going* to tell me his life story.

'As a matter of fact . . .'

He *is* telling me . . .

'. . . I'm doing a series of articles for a Sunday newspaper. Which is not really my line.'

'No?'

'I'm an academic but I have connections in Fleet Street and – well, so happened a pal of mine who's features editor, or travel editor, some such thing – I'm not up in these matters – he was in a spot. Chap he'd got doing a whole series on France . . .'

Bernard sat up.

'. . . which were so-so, we weren't *un*critical, Tina and I . . . my wife. Not uncritical. Chap was making a frightful mess of things and, apparently, he insulted the owner of the paper.'

'I remember the series, I thought it rather good. Incisive. Penetrating. Humorous.'

Adrian drew wind rapidly through his teeth. 'No, my dear

fellow, oh no! Hadn't a clue what he was on about. I lecture in French history and I know my France. And, between ourselves, my friend Monty – the editor character – he got the impression that some of the places didn't really exist. Chap had made them up!'

Bernard began to enjoy himself. 'Running a bit of a risk, surely?'

'Ex-act-lee. Just lazy I suppose. Funny how people take advantage of a good stroke of luck. I wish I'd had the French part of the assignment. However, I'm fortunate to have this.'

'You're doing the Domodossola, are you?'

'Not supposed to give it away, but you'd have guessed. Should keep my big mouth shut. Never make a real journalist.'

'I'll be interested to see what you say about it. Some of the others have similar series haven't they? I noticed something in the *Gazette*.'

'That's right. Also the *Despatch* for a while. Seems as though all the newspaper lords are trying to outdo each other. Bit childish, but who am I to complain?'

Bernard got up and smiled genially. 'What a business, this newspaper world! Glad I'm not in it.'

He went up to his room still puzzling about Fauna, and found Penny occupied with another problem. 'Darling, you can't lock the door.'

'Which door?'

'The bedroom door. There are no keys.'

'Have you asked reception.

'There's no intercom.'

'So?'

'I asked another woman I found roaming around looking for the loo and she says it's a tradition of the hotel. Everyone is on trust.'

'Christ! Sounds like a girls' boarding school.'

'We can always put a chair against the door. It's the boys I'm worried for . . .'

'They won't be disturbed. Italians are all fantastically normal.'

'How can you be so prejudiced? What about Leonardo?' Then she laughed and they fell about for a while on their high but narrow bed, until Bernard fell off. He said, picking himself up, 'More of that anon. I didn't tell you, the chap who's got my job is here. From the *Wanderer*, so try to keep our name hush-hush. He may remember it if he reads my column. We could use our aliases again?'

'*No* Bernard.'

'All right.' Bernard gave her a hug. She reacted and they found the bed wider than they had supposed.

'Wow,' said Penny when it was over, 'remember what I said about the lock.'

'We're married, aren't we?'

There was a knock at the door and Bob's voice saying, 'May I come in?' as he did just that. Penny pulled a cover quickly over her and said, 'Bob, this *isn't* Pisa.'

'I'm sorry . . .' He left instantly.

'O.K., Bob,' Bernard shouted through the door. 'What did you want?'

'I was just goin' to ask to be excused from dinner. That Rodge has invited me to join him. Quite a character. Maybe it's time he painted some locked doors.'

The dining-room at the Domodossola was in a crypt, deep in

the bowels of the hotel, reached by descending three flights of wide, stone steps. A cavernous room, it was not, however, imposing, because of the many thick piers which were the basic support of the entire building. It was an inconvenient room in which to place dining tables, and the proprietors had been driven to the not wholly happy solution of positioning many of them against a pier which then formed an obstacle between the two persons sitting either side of it, thus detracting from the intimacies of dining. Unless, that was, those two persons happened to be the Plum twins, who at once invented a game of tapping messages through the vital structure, an exercise which went on sotto voce during most of dinner. They kept their voices down against the risk of parental disapproval but there was little danger of this because the bad acoustics resulting from the low ceiling, and the many solid uprights, made it necessary for everyone to conduct their conversations at a raucously high level. The room was crowded, so the hubbub was deafening.

Penny felt as though she were in a madhouse. Isolated words and phrases reached her through the general din but she had no idea what Bernard was saying to her. She recognized Dr Mock-Templeton shrieking out names such as Caravaggio and Verrochio, and someone, as usual, in machinegun rapid Italian was repeating, maniacally, *Artoro Benedetti-Michelangeli*, over and over again. There was also an occasional roared, *Ja*! *Ja*! *Ja*! During the infrequent moments when the bellowing receded she could hear Brian in mid-fantasy tapping at the stone pier and saying hoarsely, 'I'm tunnelling through to you, Count,' and Simon replying, 'Who are you, brave fellow?'

Penny tried to concentrate on unravelling the tough piece of unfilleted and unidentifiable fish which had been placed before her.

'I'm Monty Cristo, your saviour. Keep your chin up. There's only another hundred yards of solid marble.'

'How's your fish?'

'My what?'

'*Your fish. Pesce*!'

Bernard signed to her that she should write her message down, and handed her a ballpoint, screaming, '*Write on the table cloth. It's only paper.*' But another torrent of sound burst over them so they gave up until the room began to empty and more normal exchanges became possible.

'How's your veal?'

'My what?'

'Veal.'

'This is fish,' said Penny. 'Look at the bones.'

'Mine's veal. Must be. Doesn't taste of anything.'

'*Hush*!' said Bernard commandingly and the room was committed to almost total silence, broken only by the voice of a dark-skinned man, with a thin thirties-style moustache, saying enigmatically, 'Naggio.' Seated with him was another dark-skinned man, with similarly hirsute decoration.

'So the Arabs are still with us,' murmured Bernard. 'Wonder what's happened to Fauna?'

Gideon Apthorpe-Harebrook whom he then phoned, also wondered and was displeased to hear that the Arabs had not been shaken off. 'Listen, Plum, we're all being made to look a bit foolish by that bleeder in the *Times*. He has a very humorous piece this morning about how Lord Proggle, of cheese-mountain fame, started a travel series about secluded hotels in France to impress rich society friends. And how the *Gazette* made a fool of Proggle's reporters who turned the tables on Lord Arthur himself at Cagnes. You with me, son?'

'I was there at Cagnes. And please stop calling me "son".'

'So,' Gideon went on in the same irritating tone, 'the

Times explains how the *Despatch* joined in, and how there are now four papers all trying to get in first with news of the most exclusive and secluded hotels in Italy. And how everybody is pretty bored with the whole thing except the press barons themselves . . .'

'True . . .'

'. . . who are just trying to spite each other. Don't interrupt. But it makes the further point that the *Wanderer* is offering better prizes than its rivals. Then the gossip writer sends us all up by recommending imaginary hotels in his clever way . . .'

'I could do that . . .'

'Not quite the point.'

'And I can tell you the *Wanderer*'s next hotel because I'm staying in it. And their man is here.'

'Sure, sure. One other thing. The *Evening Standard* has a story about the Arabs doing a deal direct with the Pope to get one of the missals. So that means all that has come out, and we and Proggle were trying to keep it quiet. So you have to act quickly. Vito, son.'

'But no one knows where the sodding missals are. How can the Vatican agree to sell one anyway?'

'We all have our price, son.'

As they drove into Siena next morning Bob said, 'You don't have to worry about an overcrowding situation. Guess I want to look into Tuscany a bit more. Rodge is going to show me some remarkable doors.'

'We don't want you to stay here,' said Brian.

'You come with us,' Simon added. 'This Donald's a creep. We'd rather have you.'

'That's real touching, boys, but I got a date with a madonna.'

'Hope she stands you up.'

'What an impossible place.' Bernard reversed until he reached a small square. 'How am I to get into this Pizza del Campo thing? Fly?'

'Guess you approach it from the other side, Bernie?'

'Great. *I don't happen to be coming from the other perishing side.*'

'You know what Bob means, darling.'

'It's absurd. Walled cities in this day and age. *This* way, then?'

Penny encouraged him with quiet directions, thinking, I bet Dino wouldn't make this fuss. She was instantly horrified with herself because she wasn't the unfaithful sort. She believed marriage should be lasting, that couples should try positively to make it so. She looked guiltily at Bernard and instantly thought, if he doesn't shave off that stupid beard I'll pluck it out, hair by hair. This horrified her even more.

'So we've made it. Look at that tower, boys! Magnificent!'

'Don't you think it's leaning a bit towards us, Dad?'

Penny quickly said, 'There's Donald.'

'Enchanting to see you again, dear hearts. Although my researches haven't left me much time to pine for you. The Libreria Piccolomini is out of this world. I just can't describe it. And I was treated like a V.I.P. Very flattering.' He flapped his arms in appreciation. 'And how are you, dear boys? Up to your little chins in the Renaissance, I daresay, and probably out of your depths, too. What an experience for you!'

132

'Do you have your bags ready, Donald? I'm not supposed to park here, and that palio might charge past at any moment . . .'

Donald screeched with mirth.

'We have to get going soon, to be in Rome by nightfall.'

'I think not,' said Donald. 'First we have to explore a little. There's a lake I need to visit to try to locate this missal. You know about it?'

'Yes!' they chorused.

'I've narrowed the choice down to three lakes, by clever deduction. Bolsena, Bracciano and Naggio.'

'Naggio? That's what the Arab said. That's the one, Donald.'

'We'll see,' said Donald maddeningly. 'Scholarship doesn't come out of thin air, you know. There's a process of deduction. And first, I have to take leave of my beloved Piccolomini.'

They drove to Siena cathedral and mounted the steps into the dark, heavily decorated interior. 'Not a square inch left untouched,' Bernard noted, irritably. 'I bet if you dug up one of the tiles you'd find it covered with bloody saints' heads underneath.'

Donald recognized friends. 'My dear Freda! Gemma, how delightful!'

The Misses Mock-Templeton and Brodie emerged through the gloom. Donald said, 'I was just telling my niece here about the pulpit which is by Rudolpho Pisano . . .'

'*Nicolo* Pisano,' said Freda.

'And *Giovanni*,' added Gemma.

'Assisted by Arnolfo di Cambio.'

'According to Vasari. So Berenson related.'

Bernard wished he had warned Donald that Freda Mock-Templeton was also on the missal hunt.

133

'Must get on. Where is it we're going, Pen? Oh yes, Alfarto, on Lake Bracciano.'

'The Pontormos,' screeched Gemma. 'I fainted when I first saw them. Such unusual, breath-taking use of colour. At Alfarto.' She strode up to Bernard and stared at him as though she fancied, if she stood close enough, their features might lock as in a jigsaw puzzle. He backed away and shouted unnecessarily at the boys in order to drown Donald's query about Naggio.

A priest rebuked him.

'He's telling *you* to shut up, Dad.'

Bernard ushered his party out of the cathedral but was stopped, just as the others had left its portals, by an Arab who stepped from behind a pillar.

'Sair, sair, excuse me.'

'No, I do not want filthy postcards.'

'Please. You are English.'

'Yes.'

'I look for Mr Darien Avonbury. You know him?'

'As a matter of fact we have met . . .'

'Where can I meet him?'

'I've no idea . . .'

'In Fatiyah'el Ummp we are interested in his cheese, sair.'

There was some difficulty in locating Naggio on the map because Donald had forgotten to tell the others that it was only the cognoscenti who called it that. Cartographers and compilers of guides knew it, more formally, as Rimborso di Badinaggio. Having found it at last Bernard chortled.

'You'll be glad to know that Signore Michellino refers to it as . . . *one*! *two*! *three*! . . .'

'The smiling little town of Rimborso di Badinaggio,' the Plums cried in unison, at which Donald remarked that he had always found group humour difficult to follow. As did Bernard the road. They turned off the autostrada and wound their way up a heavily wooded hillside which sparked off memories in Donald. 'How Risorgimento!'

Everyone remained aggressively silent.

'I take it,' said Donald, after a while, 'that everyone knows the story of Gioberti's sister and Garibaldi's uncle?'

'I'm not sure Brian does.'

'It was in this actual countryside . . .'

'Left or right here?' demanded Bernard.

'Map doesn't help,' said Penny.

'Garibaldi's uncle – what *was* his name? We'll call him Uncle Gari, shall we?'

Brian observed that that was better than Uncle Baldi.

'*Where Uncle Gari* met Musetta Pimento who was, as we all know, Gioberti's niece . . .'

Bernard drove away very fast and had the satisfaction of knowing that in doing so he had frightened Donald, which made that gentleman forget about the Risorgimento, although he was soon sufficiently recovered to start reminiscing about the Borgias. 'An amazing family . . . no, Simon, I didn't know any of them personally . . .' and he burbled on about them until the car reached the shores of a volcanic lake where an ancient crone sat selling strawberries. Bernard approached her, smiling. 'Lago di Naggio, signora, per favore?'

'Fragole,' she replied, 'Signore, belle fragole!' She bowed from her sitting position and waved her hands eloquently at the baskets of fruit. She then added, but Bernard could not understand her, that she would bring the blessings of the Virgin and of fourteen saints, whom she named individually, to bear upon him and his family for all time, if only he would be so kind as to purchase from her a punnet or two of strawberries, the fragrance of which was unsurpassed throughout the Appennines and even the Alps.

At a break in the performance Bernard thanked her and again asked the way to Naggio to which the old lady replied, happily wrapping exceptionally dirty newspaper around a punnet, 'Novecento lire, signore, grazie. Grazie! *Gr-aa-z-ieh*! Bella, bella!' which she went on repeating until Bernard shrugged his shoulders, handed her a bank note of huge denomination and drove off with her blessings ringing in his ears.

After a while Penny dared to say, 'We're on the wrong side of the mountain.' Almost at once the road petered out and they reached a small, pebbled car park beyond which men fished.

'Lago di Naggio?' Bernard enquired hopefully.

The fisherman slowly picked up a large trout from the bag at his side and offered it for five thousand lire.

'Nono, pesce, grazie. Io desiderare, Lago di Naggio,'

'Quattra mille lire,' the fisherman said, persuasively.

'Trota mia malattia,' Bernard responded, letting his tongue roll out repellently, and clutching his stomach in agony.

'Tre mille lire.'

'Mio non hungaria.'

'As we cannot go on, dear heart, let us return. And if I were you, Bernardo, I'd buy that trout. It looks good.'

Penny said, 'Per favore, signore, direzione lago Naggio?'

The fisherman waved his hands enthusiastically indicating that they must recirculate the lake but that before

136

doing so she would be very welcome to step into his arms.

'There is no history, I believe,' Donald said, 'of monsters in these Italian lakes, which is surprising in itself because the Italians have such vivid imaginations,' an observation soon emphasized once they had crossed the mountain and entered the smiling little town of Rimborso di Naggio. At the entrance to the lakeside settlement a placard announced that this was a place of ancient interest abounding in twelfth-century churches, thirteenth-century castles and fourteenth-century walls. It also proclaimed that the actual decayed remains of Santa Val Policella might be visited in the crypt of Santa Maria di Naggio on the Isola di Naggio in the middle of the blessed lake.

Donald remarked that the Isola was a jewel. 'We shall cross to it by boat, rowed by a lusty lad of Rimborso di Badinaggio, singing his incomparable folk tunes. But the dear Santa Val Policella had no such convenient means of transport. She arrived at the lakeside clad in nothing but rags, having walked all the way from what we now call Bulgaria . . .'

'What did they call it then?' Asked Brian.

'Rudimania,' said Donald in a voice that forbade dissent. 'It was an old Roman province. Santa Val had walked all that way, stopping only to erect a chapel here and there, and to pray with the people. When she got here to Rimborso she knew instantly she had to found an abbey . . .'

'What did she do for an abbot?' Bernard enquired.

'If you are going to make fun of the story . . .'

'You admit it's a story then?'

'Like everything in this marvellous country, legend and history are inextricably intertwined. Santa Val founded her abbey – the remains are up there on the hillside – but she hankered after more privacy . . .'

'Didn't get on with the abbot, I bet.'

'. . . more privacy, in which to worship her maker. She gazed at the little Isola and heard a voice saying. "Go there Val. Go to the little Isola and build a church".' Donald stopped, quite overcome with emotion for a moment. He rallied, 'But how was she to get across? There was no boat. *How did she do it*?' he thundered, '*Blessed Val!*'

There was a profound silence, then Simon said, 'I suppose she could have swum.'

Donald said firmly that she couldn't because of her skirt.

'I thought she was in rags,' objected Simon.

'She could have taken it off,' said Brian, and giggled.

Sternly, Donald said, 'In those days, it was more than a woman dared,' so Bernard asked what actually happened.

Donald looked elated as he began to explain. 'She picked up a rock from the hillside and said, "Friendly Stone, take me across to the little Isola". Such was her faith, that it did. She needed only an oar for which she used a sturdy branch from a fir tree. Before she knew it, she was there on the little Isola building her church. Shall we go across and see her remains?'

'We going on a rock, Donald?'

'I fear, Simon, I am a man of insufficient faith.'

'I knew he couldn't perform a miracle.'

Donald ignored these remarks and hailed a sleeping youth who sat beside a rowing boat dozing away the profitless afternoon.

'Giuseppe!' He shouted and the man slumbered on. 'Lorenzo!' he tried. Gentle snores wafted on the light breeze. Penny shouted, 'Antonio' and Bernard joined in with, 'Bassanio', but the man remained unaware of their presence.

Simon was impatient to get to the island which looked, to

him, full of possibilities for upsetting adults. He bellowed at
the comatose sailor, '*Oy woppo. Barca stola*! *Barca stola*!',
with such urgency that the man leapt to his feet actually
shouting, so Bernard liked to remember years afterwards,
'Mama Mia!'

'Simon, that wasn't polite.'

'I only told him his boat had been nicked, Mum. You can
have your phrase book back now. At least he's awake.'

The Italian, slightly aggrieved, began to negotiate terms.
'You want guide?'

'No,' said Donald. 'We know the story. Guide not
necessario.'

'I know verra good guide.'

'Bet it's your sanguinary brother-in-law.'

'He my cousin, sair.'

'We'll manage without him,' Donald said in a lordly
manner. 'Cast off!'

'I think that's a knitting term.'

'I daresay he'll know what to do. Gondoliere! Take us to
the isola, per favore.'

The boatman giggled. He fell about at the notion.

As they disembarked on the island, to the enormous
satisfaction of Roberto, the boatman, who noted that no
negotiation had taken place about a return fee, Bernard
looked back to the mainland and saw several yellow Fiats
parked near his estate wagon.

Donald led the party forward to the ancient church. 'It
almost certainly, dear hearts, underwent restoration during
the middle ages. One detects, I would think, a touch of the
quattrocento.'

'Poss-ee-ber-lay,' conceded Bernard, forgetting yellow
Fiats and their portents. 'Looking at the struc-chuar of that
tower, with all its uncompromising rectitude, I would have

thought there was a strong element of Calvinisto di Lutherano, not to mention Giovanni de Noxxo.'

Donald wished he had been blessed with an understanding of what his French friends called Le Micky-Take. Audaciously, he announced, 'I daresay the sacristan will clear all that up. Where is he?'

'Do you mean that seedy old layabout over there?' asked Bernard, unkindly, indicating an ancient person leaning against a crumbling wall and scratching at his crotch, at the same time as directing an obsequious leer at the new arrivals.

The sacristan produced an enormous bunch of rusty keys and selected one with which to unlock the swollen wooden door of the church which, groaningly, allowed itself to be dragged wide enough open for the English party to enter, but not before three emaciated native women – of indeterminate age – had rushed from behind an old yew hedge and scuttled into the dank, dark interior, crying histrionically, 'Santa Val! Santa Val!' (Only when tourists came did they have an opportunity of worshipping at their favourite shrine.)

'Reliquario,' said the sacristan, bowing them into a chapel. 'Discendere. Prudente, signora, signori. E pericoloso.' They wound their way down a narrowing stone staircase, ill-lit and without a handrail, the boys leaping ahead into the gloom, and then retreating with squeals of simulated terror. Finally they reached a mouldy chamber where, in the overpowering mustiness, a few flickering candles, recently lit by the skeletal women, indicated an area of special importance. A tattered velvet curtain was strung across a piece of flaking stone wall. The sacristan asked, did they wish to see the reliquario. Donald said, yes, of course, impatiently. The sacristan held out his hand. Donald placed several notes in it. The hand remained outstretched. Donald again obliged. The sacristan's face was still impassive. Donald pulled one thousand lire note after another out of his wallet until a slight lightness of countenance could be observed on the official's furrowed visage. A few more coins changed hands and at last keys began to jangle. A further small note did the trick and the sacristan made a totally incomprehensible speech, rising to a cackled crescendo, as he pulled the curtain aside, the corroded rings scraping along the wire spasmodically, to reveal a wizened human skull with a slightly opened mouth from which protruded one old yellow fang. The three emaciated natives fell muttering upon their knees in fervent prayer.

Penny fainted.

They found a shady seat by the lakeside and Penny sank upon it shuddering convulsively. There was no café on the island, only the church and the few semi-derelict buildings surrounding it in which dwelt the impoverished residents. The sacristan said he would fetch water which made Penny feel much worse. 'Brandy,' she pleaded. Bernard promised to do what he could, ordered the boys to stay with their mother, and went off with the sacristan.

Donald, noting with alarm the approach of another boat, asked to be excused in a tone which brooked no refusal. The boys ran off. Penny felt the healing rays of sunshine and didn't mind being left alone. She gradually gained a feeling of overwhelming peace, thinking romantically of her home in north London and of the children's school, both of which she saw in highly idealized form. She occasionally heard the voices of Brian and Simon as they played, but they did not disrupt her convalescence. All was bliss, all was calm.

Then Donald returned.

She was aware of a trembling presence close by. The table beneath which her legs were stretched began to shudder. She opened her eyes. Donald was seated next to her, obviously in a much debilitated condition.

'What is wrong? That dreadful head didn't drop off, did it?'

Donald shook his head miserably and waved his arms. 'It was so ghastly. How can I explain?'

'Try.'

'Penny, I went in there . . . oh my God!'

'Quickly,' said Penny, looking at an approaching dinghy, 'the Arabs are coming.'

'Penny, we must get away. Where are the others? Oh, my God.'

The sun went suddenly behind a cloud and the atmosphere grew unbearably oppressive. 'I will explain, but we have to get away. *Roberto*!'

The voice of Fauna Wynyates answered, as she stepped ashore with two dark-skinned men wearing khaki drill tunics and slacks. 'Think there may be a storm,' she said brightly. 'We're on a sightseeing trip.'

'Not much to see over here,' said Penny, 'which is why we are just going. Simon! Brian! Bernie!' Miraculously they all appeared just as another boat – Roberto's – arrived at the landing stage. The sound of upper-class English accents rent the air. Freda Mock-Templeton and Gemma Brodie made ecstatic noises of cultural appreciation as they stepped from the rowing-boat and observed the church, followed by Tina and Adrian Longhorn, encumbered by cameras,

142

photographic equipment and guide books, and Rodge Barnsley who took one look, not at the heavily studded door of the sacred building, but at the hardboarded addition, nailed over a rotten piece of timber, forming the entrance to the sacristan's hovel, and exclaimed, complacently, 'My next masterpiece.'

'Hello, Donald,' screeched Freda. 'Somehow thought we'd find you here.'

'We have to go,' said Donald. 'Penny is unwell. And there's going to be a storm.' He began to bargain with Roberto about a return fare and suffered severely in the outcome.

Fauna complained that it was getting crowded and asked if anyone would like to borrow their boat to get back to the mainland before they all got drenched.

'But we've only just arrived,' said Freda. 'There is much to see,' and she went purposefully towards the church.

'Come along,' urged Donald. 'Quickly! It's so bad for me to get wet.' He hustled the Plums into the waiting boat, whilst Fauna watched Freda enter the church. Rodge already had his easel up and was drawing rapidly; Adrian, more ponderously, was setting up his tripod to take a view.

The sky darkened alarmingly. The Arabs in mufti glanced uneasily towards the east as they took refuge in a Christian shrine; Adrian said to Tina, 'Where's my flash?'; and Freda, inside the church, fell over accumulated clutter in the main aisle and marvelled at such inefficiency, as the first cataclysmic burst of thunder deafened all of them.

'Cinque mille,' demanded Roberto, opening new negotiations. 'Si, si,' replied Donald, 'but get me away from here. Pronto! Pronto! *Pronto*!' He thrust a great wad of notes into Roberto's open palm, and they were at once away into the lake and making for the shore, which they did not reach before the first drenching downpour soaked them all through to their skins. They fled to Bernard's car, Roberto pursuing them because he said Donald had given him only a 'caparra'.

'Whatever that means,' said Bernard, 'we'll look it up when we've dried out.' The car windows steamed up and they all dripped lake water over the upholstery. Forked lightning streaked across the sky and Roberto crossed himself. More interestingly, so did Donald.

Bernard gave Roberto a large note and the boatman, recovering his composure immediately, despite another impressive display of lightning with attendant drumrolls of thunder, advised a quick dash to a nearby hotel. 'My bruzza has it. Verra good.'

They didn't argue but leapt out and through the cascading rain into a damp-smelling edifice which, nevertheless, had the evident advantage of a non-leaking roof.

After dinner Donald explained.

'It is time,' he choked out, looking despondently on the flooding exterior of the hotel, 'for me to make my miserable confession.'

'What have you been up to? Didn't you find your old missal?'

'Don't, *don't*, Penelope. You have no idea of what I've been through!'

'Then why doesn't he tell us?' Simon said to Brian.

'This is not for young ears. Dear heart, perhaps the boys should go to bed . . .'

Loud protests were not overruled because Penny felt she would like the family to stay together in such menacing weather. Simon and Brian were told to keep quiet and not interrupt. 'Now then, Donald, tell us all.'

'After you had been taken ill, I returned to the church. I

was certain that if the missal were there, it would be in the vestry. It was terribly difficult getting the vestry door open, I don't think anyone had been in there for centuries. I had to put my shoulder to it and it came off one hinge when I did, but that's of no account. Oh my God, what will happen to me!' Donald covered his face with his hands and wailed.

'What happened to the missal?' asked Bernard impatiently.

'Dear heart, don't ask me! It disintegrated!'

'Did you see it do that?' Penny enquired stupidly.

'I'm telling you, and I'd taken such care . . .'

'So it *was* in the vestry?'

'I walked into the murky interior and at first I couldn't see a thing. There were trees and bushes growing against the windows, which were filthy anyway. And there was just one shaft of sunlight breaking through. When I got used to the darkness I could see a big chest. I opened it and it was full of rotting vestments. Then I noticed a cupboard above it. That's where it was. The missal. Lying on a piece of old blue velvet very much moth-eaten, I may say, and under a glass case. I lifted it down very gingerly and placed it on a table. The case was padlocked but when I picked up the lock, experimentally, it just fell off.'

'Lucky you.'

'Wait. As it fell it jerked the glass cover, which fell off the table and smashed. But at least I could see the missal which had very tiny splinters of glass dropped on it but I don't think they did much damage. I examined the missal and found it had got pages of illuminated manuscript – very beautiful, they looked, so I got out my light meter and flash and I took some photographs. Then I thought, where was it printed? Many of these incunabulae didn't have title pages you know. This one didn't but sometimes the printer put his name at the back. As in this case, on the last page. It was printed in Rouen in 1496. I was so excited, that I couldn't resist picking the dear thing up, holding it. That's when it happened. It was too much for it. The handling and the flashlight, even the sunlight, after all those years. It just fell to pieces. Disintegrated. The pages cascaded over the floor, some of them reduced to pellets as they fell . . .'

'Fancy them knowing about built-in obsolescence all that time ago.'

'It lasted nearly five hundred years Bernard. Now, through my foolishness, it is destroyed. Do you think I shall be charged?'

'With what?'

'Destroying an ancient monument.'

'They don't seem to have looked after it very well themselves. I don't see,' Bernard went on, 'how you can prove now that it was the missal you were looking for.'

'I can if my photos come out, but then I shall have to confess.'

'More sensible if we pretend we haven't found it, and get off to Frascati and find the other one.'

'Not tonight, dear heart. I just hope,' Donald added insincerely, 'that our friends on the Isola are all right.'

'You can't even see it, the rain's so thick,' said Penny.

'Won't Roberto go over to rescue them?' asked Brian.

'In this hurricane, you must be mad,' retorted his brother.

'He'd have to if he were a proper lifeboatman, like Grace Darling . . .'

'He isn't . . . anyhow, she wasn't . . .'

The storm raged on and didn't play itself out until daybreak, soon after which Roberto crossed to the island and brought back the English party. Neither Freda nor Gemma was much perturbed by the ordeal they had endured

146

but the Longhorns were in poor shape.

'What happened to the other party?' Bernard asked. 'I thought that that Fauna Wynyates woman was there with a couple of Arabs.'

'They went immediately, after you,' said Freda indifferently. 'One thing, Donald, I must tell you. There's no harm in letting you in on a little secret. I was here because I was hoping to discover a certain rare book which it was whispered to me . . .'

'Why were you looking for it?'

'I'm a Russian spy, didn't you know?' Freda said jocularly, very gratified at having caused such reaction in Donald. 'Anyhow, if the book was there before the storm, it ain't now. Think I must have got the wrong island.'

Donald recovered and felt intense relief. The storm must have destroyed all evidence of his criminal act. And, he thought unworthily, now I have the only photographs of the missal, and there can never be any more. He began to muse over the possibilities of even greater glory if only he could get his hands on the one at Frascati. 'I'm feeling much better,' he said to Bernard. 'I think we should leave at once.'

As they passed reception Darien Avonbury was asking the patron if a Miss Fauna Wynyates happened to be in residence.

'Hasn't been seen since the storm,' said Bernard.

'Hello, old son. You know her, of course.'

'She's in with the Arabs now. Doesn't seem to be working for Proggle any more. Incidentally, I came across an Arab who was very anxious to meet you. In Siena.'

Darien looked self-deprecating. 'In my position, all sorts of people seek me out.'

'He wants to buy your cheese mountain.'

'There's no need to be offensive.'

'Seriously. Said he represented Fatiyah'el Ummp.'
'Where the hell's that?'
'Try the third oasis on the right.'

'We're being followed again,' Bernard said, noting three yellow Fiats keeping their distance behind him. For some miles he amused himself exceeding the speed limit, always assuming there was one, and then slowing down to a dawdle. Once, to his satisfaction, he saw one Fiat moving into the outside lane to avoid hitting another.

Simon rummaged around and found his telescope. 'I think it's those dark men, Dad, in the car behind.'

'The Aye-rabs, really?'

'And there's a lady in one of them.'

'Anyone we know?'

'It think it's the one Donald calls Freda.'

They continued down the autostrada, in procession. Once or twice Bernard turned down a side road and drove through a few towns and villages, but the Fiats followed, so he settled for leading them all into Rome and there, he hoped, losing them in the thick of the traffic.

'We'd better buy papers as soon as we get there, Donald, and see what the opposition are up to. I'm sure it's time Trafford Thing put in a reappearance. We haven't seen him since Cagnes, and we know he's at work for the *Despatch*.'

They crossed the ring road encircling Rome, and made for the centre. Bernard noticed a young woman with a pram tentatively stepping on to a pedestrian crossing, and pulled up. The effect was even worse than it would have been in

France. There was the sound of one hundred vehicles braking in unison, a smell of burning rubber; angry shouts were heard, and then he was aware of grinding, revving noises and of fists being shaken at him, as those who had been following swept by on the wrong side. Miraculously the lady with the pram had reached the opposite pavement unharmed and was smiling appreciatively. Slightly shaken, he drove on, saying, 'When in Rome is all very well . . . but I don't know if I dare drive as the Romans do.'

'They,' said Penny, 'have the advantage of being in little Fiats. This minibus of ours is too large to play at Brands Hatch.' Their hotel, like its famous neighbour the Villa Borghese, had once been a palace. To enter, they mounted a huge baroque staircase with giant porpoises, threatening bemused maidens, carved all over its balustrades. The vestibule was as large as the booking hall of a major railway terminus and there was sculpture everywhere, adorning the marble pillars supporting the huge structure – sculpture with a marine theme. Dolphins and fish from mythology swirled around the columns, dangled from the roof and emerged from the floor. It was the same in the dining-room where Penny examined the menu, deciding the proprietor was an anglophile, which was pleasant even though he hadn't mastered her language.

'We can have boiled hen, with mixed contours. That should be nice.'

'What actually is it?'

'Or there's fumed sammons. Wasn't he a violinist?'

'I'm not sure about the lamb cuntlets,' said Bernard. 'Shall I have them or the barren English bif?'

'Fish dishes are interesting,' Penny observed. 'They're listed under the heading "*Pesky*". How about sozzled mackeroon, for a starter?'

Donald dissociated himself. To the charming, black-haired waiter with flashing white teeth, he said airily that he desired Insalata di Finocchi e cetrioli.

'In-sa-la-ta de Fin-occ-hi e cet-ri-oli' repeated the waiter in a descant. 'No sir, I see. I think we not have it.'

'What?'

'Is Italian dish.'

'Well?'

'We have English dish. Verra good beef.'

Donald sighed. 'So have I come all this way for the roast beef of old England?'

'England verra nice,' said the beaming waiter. 'I work some year in Bristol. Is verra nice, Bristol. But too many foreigners, I think.'

'In Bristol?' queried Bernard. 'Really?'

'Yes sir, too many Welsh, Irish, Scotchmen. I like English.'

'How very nice of you,' said Penny. 'What's your name?'

'Paolo, signora.'

'I shall call you Paul.'

'Thank you, signora.'

'Some white wine, please, Paul. A nice dry white.'

'No, sir, no white wine.'

'*No white wine*!'

'White wine, finito. Finish. Have verra nice beer . . .'

Waiting on the platform for the Frascati train they heard a tannoy announcement which left even the natives puzzled. Most people ignored it and went on reading their newspapers. One or two looked anxiously round for an official to pester.

'Wonder what all that was about, Bernie?'

'The only word I could recognize,' said Simon, 'was cancellare.'

'All I heard as usual was artoro-benedetti-michel-angeli-pronto-spaghetti. They never say anything else, apart from ravioli-incastrati. Cancellare, did you say, Simon?'

'I think that's what he said. What's it mean?'

'Cancelled, thickhead. They've cancelled the train.'

'Then why are all these people still waiting for it?' Brian asked.

'Perhaps,' said Simon, 'they were saying they hadn't cancelled it.'

'Why should they make an announcement to say they haven't cancelled a train?' Bernard said crossly. 'You don't go around saying trains which everyone expects to run *haven't* been cancelled.'

'Perhaps *they* do,' said Simon doggedly.

'Shut up, Simon.'

The tannoy suddenly blasted forth again. This time the natives all sighed and shouted at each other resignedly, then tramped off the platform in the direction of the main station. The Plums followed them. 'But,' said Penny, alarmed, 'they are walking across the track. Surely that's not allowed?'

'Don't say when in Rome . . .' Donald threatened, 'or I'll scream.'

'You'll do more than that if you tread on the live rail.' Donald jumped involuntarily and caught his foot between two sleepers as he touched down again. 'Now,' he complained, 'I suppose I have to stand here and be mown down by the Oriental express as it roars through!

'We must hope it won't,' said Bernard, 'because this is a

terminus. Try taking your foot out of the shoe. And just to reassure you, there isn't a live rail; the cables are overhead.'

'How silly of you to frighten me.' Donald wrenched at his shoe as a loud blast on a horn sounded and the lights of a nearby engine flashed on and off.

'Something wants to come by,' said Simon.

'It's our train, I think,' added Brian.

Donald freed his shoe and they all clambered onto the platform, Bernard shouting at a porter, 'Frascati?'

'Si, signore.'

'Pronto?'

The train slowly began to move.

'Si, signore.'

'Prego.'

'Prego, signore.'

'Thank you. Prego.'

The train wound slowly out of the station and with every sign of imminent collapse began the long ascent to Frascati.

'Wouldn't surprise me to learn that Hadrian travelled on this thing. It looks about the same age as the aqueduct which keeps passing us,' said Bernard, looking to the boys for appreciation of his joke which Donald spoilt by remarking, 'I don't think it can be correct to say the aqueduct is passing us; surely we are passing it . . .'

'Point taken. Now what about the missal you're bent on destroying today?'

'Dear heart, don't say such a thing. This is purely an exploratory trip, assuming we get there.' The train ground to a halt between high hedges, and then started as it intended to go on, in a series of jolts, so that Donald and Bernard – seated on opposite sides of the compartment – were jerked forwards and backwards to and from each other with every lurch, like badly gloved puppets. When it eventually made Frascati,

152

Bernard decided to let Donald do his business alone and announced that he would devote the afternoon to the entertainment of his sons, towards which end he instantly sat down at the nearest café table and ordered ice cream for them and the local white wine for Penny and himself. A surly waiter, heavily influenced by a succession of visits from English beatniks dressed in denim, and scarcely visible beneath flowing strands of hair, said there wasn't any white wine. 'Finito.' Penny said she'd rather have lemon tea anyway. That was also finito. Penny and Bernard watched their sons consume buckets of ice cream, after which they walked about the town, thinking how fortunate they were to be free of Donald. 'If he were here we'd have to suffer an endless lecture on local history. Of course, it is actually terribly interesting this place. The Etruscans were here first you know, and Bonnie Prince Charlie . . .'

'Da-ad!' Complained the boys in unison.

Bernard sat them down at another café and shouted, 'Cameriere! Une caraffa de vino blanco, *locale*.'

'Finito,' said the waiter, waving his hands eloquently.

'Perhaps you would direct me to the nearest grape,' Bernard complained bitterly. Almost immediately his attention was distracted by Donald, who appeared agitated. 'I told you. He's loused it up again.'

'I've met them all,' cried Donald. 'They're all here. What are we to do?'

'Sit down and explain yourself.'

'What is there to drink?'

'Drink, I have to inform you, is finito. There's a world shortage.'

Donald groaned and Bernard told him to pull himself together. 'There's always your hip flask. Think how it is for Penny and me. Mine's in the car.'

Donald did as he was bid and said he had been prowling around in the piazza by the little church at the back of Frascati, the one where the missal was known to be, when suddenly he was surrounded by English people. 'I recognized all of them. And most of them as enemies. That Trafford was there and his so-called wife, Annabelle. And the dashing young lady who escorts the Arabs. And those Shorthorns . . .'

'Longhorns.'

'Not to mention Freda and Gemma. And they all seemed to be working for different organizations but to be ganging up in order to get in and see the missal. And they were all absolutely outraged because . . . what do you think?'

'Go on.'

'The priest in charge won't accept a tip. He is really incorruptible. I can't tell you how dismayed they are.'

'Weren't you?'

'No, I'd heard he was straight already. That's why I need time to work out something.'

'Cameriere!'

'Si, signore.'

'Vino rosso, per favore.'

'Finito, signore.'

Bernard groaned as Donald wailed, what was he to do? 'This is such an opportunity.'

'On this hill of temperance, surrounded by fields of withering vines, about the only thing I can think of is that you become a nonconformist parson.' Bernard brightened. 'Yes, that's it. Become a priest. Get in there with a big dog collar on.'

154

'I must give credit where credit is due,' pontificated Donald as they all examined the menu that evening and settled on Carousel of Cock in Fungi Sauce. 'I've not often felt moved to praise you, Bernard – we do not always see, as you would say, oeil-à-oeil – but that was a touch of inspiration suggesting I should dress up as a holy man. It has meant complete success for my mission, although we must be careful to go on fooling the others for a while yet. Did you have a satisfactory day, dear heart?'

'Fair. I met Darien Avonbury again. Apparently the Government forbade the cheese deal with the Chinese but it was too late. It had already been shipped. There is some talk of intercepting the ship before it reaches Chinese waters, which would make for a fine old international incident; but Darien seems confident in his usual superior way. But nobody really cares about it all except a few back benchers. And *Tribune* and the National Front.'

'I cannot understand, Bernard-O, why the Chinese want this cheese.'

'I bet they don't. I wouldn't put it past them to sell it back to the Italians.'

'But, dear heart, it's their cheese in the first place.'

'I know. What a story this is going to make. You see, it's still cheaper for the supermarkets here to buy it from the Chinese.'

'Surely, it's illegal?'

'There are ways round, apparently.'

'Aren't economics baffling? So, we're all getting what we want. I say, shall we celebrate and have something rather special with the meal tonight? You know, champers? I can't tell you how much I've enjoyed being a cardinal.'

'I suppose that's why you're still wearing your dog collar, your eminence.'

'Am I really, Penny? Well, I can't remove it here in the dining-room. I'll carry the whole thing off. Perhaps I'll be an archbishop next week. Now what about lovely bubbly?'

Champagne was, of course, off, but they had asti spumante instead which, said Donald, was quite good enough for the sort of meal they were eating.

'So, tomorrow, Penny, sweety – boys – Donald . . . we start on the last stage of the trip to Venice. Where better to end so exhilarating an adventure?'

'I suppose,' said the cardinal, 'the paper can't afford the Danieli?'

'You're joking. But I have a place lined up on the lagoon where the scampi is said to be the best in Europe. The chef was somewhere fabulous in Bologna for twenty years. And I'm told there's nothing in the toe and heel of Italy to touch it.'

'Bliss, what bliss, dear hearts . . .' Donald stopped and appeared worried by something he had observed through the window. 'I swear to you that that nun who passed by was that girl Annabelle. And the priest with her was Trafford. They must be up to the same lark.'

'In that case I am utterly convinced I saw one of the Ay-rabs dressed as a monk when I was coming down to dinner.'

Further reflection was prevented by the dramatic arrival of Leonardo Giovanni Dino-dino Caradente-Vecchio who had sensational news. 'Vesuvio,' he proclaimed. 'It erupts tonight.'

'Can we go, Dad?'

'Ah-ha,' said Dino, 'like the great fireworks display, you think. But very dangerous. Is better you stay.'

Bernard asked what actually had occurred.

'There is this report from the three scientists who were there working in the crater. They have come out. They very

156

worried. Have told the government . . .' He made graphic gestures indicative of explosion, destruction, total calamity.

'Is there an evacuation order?'

'Not yet, but everyone very worried in Napoli, Castellamare, Pompeii . . . especially Pompeii.'

Bernard phoned Gideon and, for once, was not rebuffed.

'Get down there at once, and when it starts erupting give us an eye-witness account from Pompeii or Herculaneum. *Eye-witness* account.'

'Look here, I'm not a war correspondent.'

'Aren't you?' said Gideon. 'I was.'

Bernard, feeling something of a poltroon, bade Penny and the boys farewell, and set off down the inferior autostrada to Napoli wishing, not for the first time, that he could edit a column of news and views from the comfort of his study overlooking the River Pymmes at Osidge.

When he had departed Donald said he would make it his business to inform the other journalists of the expected cataclysm so that their attention might be diverted from the missal hunt. 'It would help to have them all down in the Bay of Naples, red herring fishing.'

'Is it a red herring, Donald?'

'This sort of rumour has been occurring for years, Penny. Paolo, dear fellow, there you are at last. Now don't tell me that coffee is off, or I shall swoon in my wily wizened way. Due cappucini, yes?'

'No, sir. Maxwell House. Verra good. Named after great

English politician.'

After seeing the boys to bed Penny felt unaccountably cross with Bernard. What was he doing racing through the night to a possible danger zone and abandoning them once again? This was no pattern for family life.

She thought she should undress and get into bed, but she wasn't tired, and it was hot and stuffy. Outside it was a splendid balmy night and, for the first time in her life, she was in Rome. If Bernard hadn't frantically driven away they might have walked about the fabled city together in the moonlight.

At least she could enjoy the hotel terrace, to which she descended, past the giant porpoises threatening the bemused maidens, not in a mood of rhapsodical adulation, but in one of sullen revolt. She was tired of being abroad and longed for the familiar comforts of the spacious flat in Osidge, and of the lush garden attaching thereto which was, no doubt, by now hideously overgrown with convolvulus, speedwell, plantain, dandelions and ground elder. She sat on a marble couch, then rose quickly and walked to the end of the balcony where she stood for a while leaning against the dorsal fin of some enormous sculptured sea creature as she watched the lights twinkling in the grounds of the Villa Borghese.

'It is very beautiful, I think.'

She turned to be confronted by Dino who said, 'I am a Florentine. I am modern Renaissance man, yes? But also, I love Roma. As my great forebear Michel Angelo did.'

Penny laughed. 'You're descended from Michaelangelo?'

'Of course.'

'But *truly* . . .?'

'All true Italians, dear lady, are descended from Michel Angelo.'

'You are all incurably romantic. Dino?'

'Signora?'

'Will you take me for a walk into Rome, please? Now, I mean.'

Which was how Penny, faithful and loving wife of Bernard Plum, came to spend part of that balmy night with Leonardo Giovanni Dino-dino Caradente-Vecchio, whilst her husband, approaching the Bay of Naples in the small hours, sat in his car in a lay-by, dozing fretfully, as giant trucks thundered by.

Dino, resourceful man, knew a way into the Forum by night, and conducted Penny around the shadowy ruins of ancient Rome, and up into the Farnese Gardens where they crunched gently along the gravelled paths until they rested awhile on a bench where she allowed him to kiss her.

She had certainly not been kissed like that before, and, in a dream, she allowed Dino to lead her away from the Forum, past the huge Colosseum, and into a carossa, pulled by an old nag nearly as tired as she was herself. At the hotel she made only the feeblest objection to entering his bedroom – she was too fatigued to know what she was about (so she told herself next day) – but once she was in his bed she quickly realized she was with a man very different from Bernard, who was easily roused and satisfied, although he usually reached his climax before hers. Dino romped her about the bed, first on top of her, then underneath, now at her side, now holding her backwards over the foot of the bed and making to enter her. Then pulling back and allowing himself to fall sideways off the wide divan, clutching her desperately to him.

Now they were back firmly in the centre with the springs squeaking and he was creeping slowly up her body, his hard tool thumping against her stomach, then beating on her breasts, her neck, her chin, until, with distaste, she realized he wished to thrust it into her mouth. He was utterly surprised when she hurled him away with unexpected strength, so that he had to come against the bedhead before falling on to the sheets.

'I'm sorry. I don't like that sort of thing.' She grabbed her negligée and fled down the corridor leaving an outraged Dino, naked in the doorway, crying, 'Bitch! English whore! I get you!'

Penny couldn't remember her room number and ran into a bathroom where, dismayed, she noted that was no key to turn in the lock. She heard several doors opening and closing and people shouting, 'pronto', 'prego' and 'lento'. Then all was quiet and she thrust a chairback under the door handle and sat on the bathroom stool until daybreak, thinking miserably of Bernard, who at that moment was booking into a seedy hotel near the entrance to Pompeii Antica, and endeavouring, in the early morning mist, to make out in which direction lay the fearsome volcano.

At the entrance to the ruins various ragged and importunate youngsters entreated Bernard to buy cigarettes, dope and 'dolls which you can really fuck, signore'. He refused them all and asked a uniformed attendant to point out Vesuvius to him. The man said it was above the cloud. 'When you see it, sair, it means a-rain.'

'Just like Bexhill.'

'Yes sair.'

Bernard handed over two ragged pieces of paper representing 200 lire for this information, and made for the ruins where he hoped to meet someone in authority. On a previous visit he recalled a museum. So there must be a curator who would surely know about the expected eruption – unless he had already packed and gone. Yet there was no sign of panic and he certainly didn't wish to provoke one. If the thing did start spouting fire he would make a quick getaway up the autostrada, and bugger Gideon Apthorpe-Harebrook.

He went to the ticket office where they demanded 150 lire. Recklessly he had given his last small notes to the man who had told him Vesuvius couldn't be seen so he pulled out a 10,000 lire note which made the Ingreso-wallah shake his head. 'Smaller, signore?'

Bernard offered a British 2p piece, two boiled sweets, a crumpled picture postcard of the Arno at Pisa, and a grubby comb with many teeth missing. None of these was acceptable so he said he would write a cheque backed by a credit card. This was frowned upon.

He offered Access and Barclay, Diners and American Express. None would do. Then he had an idea and pulled out a petrol coupon purchased from the A.A. to lessen the cost of fuel in Italy. The Ingresso-man leapt and snatched it slightly ahead of two of his compatriots. Bernard received as change a bag of sweets and a metal disc for use in a telephone booth.

The museum was closed; which made Bernard suppose the rumoured eruption was true, but it was only an instance of current policy which made for a shortage of staff because of lack of money to pay them. So, with no curator to nobble, he trotted up the cobbled causeway to the forum wishing he could remember the difference between an atrium and a peristyle.

He wandered awhile, deliberately taking any direction in which a conducted tour wasn't going, but wishing he had bought a printed guide. At the end of a long street of excavations he went through a modern metal gateway, attached to a well-preserved piece of ruin, and found himself in a courtyard where grapes were growing abundantly above stone trellis work. There were many chambers and passageways to explore and, for a while, he forgot he was supposed to be covering a new eruption and lost himself in the pleasure of ruins. He sat down in an alcove and surveyed the tranquil scene of ancient devastation before him. Then he heard an unattractively familiar voice somewhere behind him saying, 'And you – ah – would deliver the – ah – cheese to – ah – Fattiya al Summp – ah?'

'No need, please. Too much expense. We bling straight here.'

'But – ah – I mean – ah – ah – dangerous. This E.E.C. Common – ah – Market.'

'Not vlorry, please. We see Lord Flountainshorn. He advliser for Sheikh. Now please. Phlotograph. Pleople come.'

Bernard felt very professional indeed, as Gideon listened with what could be taken as respect, as he related a story of Lord Proggle being involved with the ex-Chairman of the National Cheese Board in selling back to the Italians their own produce. It couldn't be all that long now before Fleet Street bestowed on him his due. Rees-Mogg would be well advised to look to his laurels . . .

162

Back in Rome, Dino, who had always understood that most English women were suffering deprivation because of the blinkered attitude of their menfolk towards the more exciting variations of sexual intercourse, was furious that Penny had rejected him. His attempt at oral intercourse was only a feint as she should have realized. He did not wish the moment of orgasm whilst his weapon was in her mouth. It was his great finesse to remove it from the lips just in exquisite time to plunge it into the appropriate place, so that they should both have sublime delight. This she had denied him in her prudish way. She had humiliated him. What was he to do?

It was her husband who must suffer, which he already had by being sent to Pompeii in the middle of the night. Imagine his news editor falling for such a story that Vesuvio was about to erupt! Although there was unwelcome irony in the way he had erupted himself. Never mind, there would be other women, other times, although he did feel attracted to this Penny. He would like to teach her a thing or two.

Meanwhile, what was happening to the cheese mountain? There was more to the issue, he was convinced, than mere cheese, and it was this he must uncover. He must give it his total attention and then, perhaps, conquer the English lady later.

Bernard could not countenance a second night in the sleazy hotel at Pompeii, and moved round the bay to pleasant quarters in a Victorian hotel on the Piano di Sorrento, where he took a balcony room from which he could see the mist over Vesuvius. He was much amused as he sauntered through the markets to catch glimpses of Trafford and various Arab familiars, all no doubt still in desperate pursuit of the lost missal. As he sipped a cold beer on his balcony in the late evening he thought of how it was all working out his way.

Then he looked across the bay and became aware of astonishing happenings. The sky was brilliant with light. It was erupting. My god, he thought, I really am here, two thousand years later and witnessing what old Pliny saw . . . I think it was Pliny. Before the actual lines of communication were penetrated by solid lava he must get through to London. He laid thousands of lire on the hotel reception desk as tribute and bade them dial for him. At last Gideon answered.

'It's erupting, Gid. Plum here. I'm not actually at Pompeii . . . I'm sorry, that's shut. But I'm here in Sorrento watching it across the bay. And the lava's falling. The whole of Naples will soon be engulfed.'

'Yes,' said Gideon curtly. 'Well, we have our own problems here just now. Give us a call in the morning.'

Bernard drove swiftly to Rome, up the badly maintained autostrada. He had never been so conned in all his life. Why had those fool students from Napoli chosen that night to light their bonfire on the edge of Vesuvio? And how had Gideon known so soon, and why had he sounded so indifferent? At least he could console himself by knowing that he and Donald had tied up the missal business. Now they could get on and enjoy Venice before setting out for home, which would be very welcome in itself. He was bored with abroad.

In Rome he found Penny weepy and curiously unable to cope with the boys.

'Bernie, I've been . . . I'm sorry. Oh God, it's so lovely to have you back.' She clutched him, even caressing his despised little beard.

'It was all right, Pen. There wasn't any danger. It was a hoax. I was made to look a bit foolish but, fortunately, for some reason, Gideon-thing didn't seem to want to know . . .'

'Darling, I do love you. I do. Don't let anyone say I don't.'

Bernard was touched. He caressed her and wished it was a more appropriate moment to do more, but the boys were present. 'I love you too, Pen. Won't it be nice to get home after all this? We've been away too long. Think I'll have a wash down. Feel very mucky after that drive.'

He went into the bathroom and took a shower. He noticed himself in the handbasin mirror as he was drying himself. God, he was a mess. All shaggy. How lucky that Pen still loved him. On an impulse he shaved off his beard.

They had travelled from the Schiavoni to the railway station, and Donald had told them, in detail, about the palaces on the left bank of the grand canal. They had had drinks and ice cream – amazingly little was finito in Venice – and clicked cameras. They had been short-changed on five occasions, since arriving on the lagoon, but they were not embittered because it was all too entrancing and different from anything they had seen before. Even the prospect of Donald resuming his lecture as they set out on the return canal trip by vaporetto didn't dampen their high spirits. They didn't have to listen.

At the railway station landing stage the vaporetto tied up and one swarm of Venetians charged off the craft to collide with another swarm boarding it. Somehow individual aims were all achieved without anyone falling into the water. The Plums and Donald were gently buffeted towards the prow, which vantage point, Donald assured them, was essential if he were to conduct his lecture without constantly moving from port to starboard and back as the vaporetto traversed the canal.

'Now we are about to pass the greatest treasure of all – the Queen of the Palazzos – Palazzi – the Ca' d'Oro, the golden house, it means. I don't mind confessing that I have sometimes wept as I looked at it . . .'

'How many windows has it got?' asked Brian but before Donald could respond the voice of Freda Mock-Templeton was heard braying above his. 'Of carse, the pictures are quite out of this world. You know the Titian – Il Tiziani, should I say, in this city of cities?' She laughed up a whole scale. '*Venus with a Looking Glass*? No? Oh, Adrian, what you have missed. You must winkle your way in. And don't forget, if you do, to remark the Lippi – Filip*pino* Lippi that is, of carse.'

'Of course,' said Adrian with a mirthless bared teeth smile, so set that his wife wondered if he might have had a stroke. Adrian, who hadn't, just wished Freda would speak more softly because everyone was looking at him, which was quite contrary to the effect Dr Mock-Templeton wished to achieve, which was to have everyone look at her. At least Brian had the correct reaction. 'There's that lady,' he cried.

'*Mi-iss*! *Oy-ee*!'

Freda, unable to pretend she had not heard the greeting, turned and smiled frostily at Brian. 'Hello, young laddie,' she said with some inspiration, knowing Brian would hate being thus addressed, to which he retorted, 'How many windows has it got?'

'That's a good question. How many bays, we say, don't we in architectural terms?'

'Freda,' bawled Donald. 'How you do follow us around. Now the next palace, boys, is the Casa della Maltesa. It once belonged to the King of Prussia but I must confess I am not sure who owns it now.'

'I do,' said Adrian, loudly. 'I mean, we do.' He blushed.

'You must have done jolly well out of Proggle,' said Bernard, outraged.

'Nothing to do with that,' said Adrian. 'We sold our house in Hertfordshire for rather a lot.' He looked self-conscious. 'It's become part of a complex which is the base for the Anglo-Arab League of Friendship.'

'You might say,' added Tina, 'that we made a sacrifice in a very noble cause.'

'I wonder what our friend Vesoul made out of it,' Bernard said to Donald. 'I bet it's him.'

'Talking of Proggle, have you heard the news?' asked Adrian, who wished to change the subject. 'He's endowed the church at Frascati with oodles of loot in return for the missal, which he is presenting to the Vatican, for its own collection. Or, at the Pope's discretion, to be sold to the highest bidder. Anyway, he should get his Papal decoration now.'

It was interesting to note that all their old rivals were booked into the same hotel on the lagoon. 'What does it matter?' said Penny. 'We've won. It's just unpleasant to have to be civil to that Anabelle and Trafford after all they did to us.'

Eventually they all moved into the dining-room, in the centre of which was a large round table occupied by Lord Arthur Proggle and friends. The Fountainshorns were there, also Darien Avonbury, and Pilgrim Tolmers. Fauna Wynyates and her Arabs were seated with them, and the Longhorns too.

As the Plums and Donald took a nearby table Darien Avonbury was raising a crystal goblet and saying, 'Eva! My dear! May I drink to the success of your new book, and wish you the greatest ever success?'

'Darien, how enchanting. It's only a trifle really.' She blushed with pleasure and her husband quickly changed the subject. After all, he hadn't read the book. 'I think it was here, was it not Eva, that we once ate fettuccine in agrodolce?'

'Christ, I do 'ope it didn't hurt,' said Bernard, intending to be overheard. 'But in any case, Penny darl, I'm going to have an absolute mazurka of a moussaka, this night.' He waved patronizingly at Ted.

Arthur Proggle wished they'd all shut up so he could make his momentous announcement; after all, he was paying. With malicious approval he noted that Bernard Plum, who had thrown camomile tea in his face, was seated nearby. His lips parted in sparse pleasure.

'Any road,' said Ted, regaining his equanimity, 'Tonight I shall be into Alfonso's scampi alla laguna. Sheer lunacy to come here and ignore it. No one tittilates his scampi like Alfonso.'

Proggle could contain himself no longer. 'Listen

everybody,' he snapped, rising and clapping his hands to attract attention. They all turned and stared in amazement. Whatever, thought Ted, has got into squirty little Arthur?

'Listen,' said Proggle. 'You must all be the first to know.' It was the master touch of the lord of the media. *They* were to be the custodians of a well-kept secret. They listened. The Plums and Donald also listened.

'It's already got out that I'm presenting His Holiness with the Frascati muzzle, and I think our friends from Oy' el Summp will be glad to know that His Holiness has accepted their offer to buy it . . .' There was polite, discreet applause. The Arabs looked as though they expected to be swindled at some time between the main course and the dessert but, resolutely, remained impassive.

'What none of you don't know,' said Lord Proggle, 'is that I have also made another purchase . . .'

'Not the cheese, for Christ's sake,' Ted said audibly to Darien.

'*I have bought* . . .'

'The Arabs have paid cash for that, Ted . . .'

'*I have bought* . . .' He brought his fist down hard on the table, shaking crockery, spilling wine '. . . the *Gazette*.'

Bernard said, 'Oh, no.'

'What's more . . .'

He had their attention now.

'. . . You'll understand this means spending a lot of money. Has to be financed. Even I couldn't manage it alone. So I want you to know I've sold a substantial interest in the *Sabbatical* empire to the Sheikh of Oy'el Pie'eep.'

Donald, alone, looked entirely happy.

169

The Plums retired, despondent, to their room. Donald, before following them, went on to the terrace where he was soon joined by Fauna Wynyates who complained that Proggle, over excited with his disclosures, had taken to wine again, and become objectionable.

'Pawing all over me, he was. And in front of everyone. I really couldn't stand it. He has no finesse.'

Donald excused himself. He did not feel up to comforting the lady who was joined soon after by Dino.

'Buona sera, signora,' he said automatically, noticing a female presence close by. They fell into polite conversation, which became more animated as the shadows thrown by Fauna's figure worked on Dino's imagination. Quite quickly he discovered she was English and connected with Lord Proggle. Skilfully, he led the conversation around to the cheese mountain.

Instantly Fauna scoffed. 'Cheese,' she said. 'It has nothing to do with cheese.'

Dino grew amorous as he divined that Fauna had the key to the story he wished to break upon the world. She allowed him to be, having been short of a man for longer than she cared to remember, and finding his close proximity extremely provocative.

'What is it, about you English women?' asked Dino.

She snuggled up to him and said that surely he knew.

He played up to her and they entwined themselves harmlessly together as he, boldly asking if he could dare to compare himself with Lord Proggle as a possible lover, was given the blatant truth not only on that score, but also on the matter which, regrettably, interested him, for once, more than the charms of conquest.

Before they reached Dino's bed he had learned what he wanted to know but thought it only proper to conclude what he saw as a bargain. In any case, the lady intrigued him. As he certainly intrigued Fauna, when she felt him working up her body. This she had longed for. She had had men before but only in a straightforward way. She had always hoped for something kinky and as he drew close to her lips she felt ready for her own climax. Then, inexplicably, he withdrew and was trying to penetrate her. She threw him aside in fury and leaped from his bed, and his room.

Dazed, Dino sat alone, wondering what it was about English women that he repelled them so.

Penny was not on her best navigational form after they had crossed the Alps. Bernard had asked her to make for Bourg and, stupidly, she thought he had meant Bourges. Donald had, again, mysteriously disappeared since their instant dismissal by Proggle, following his purchase of the *Gazette*. Added to which Bernard was the victim of extreme self-pity and she couldn't rouse him from it. Since leaving Venice he had insisted that they must all tighten their belts. There was no prospect of a job and they needed to save every penny. The car could be taken from them at any moment if Proggle remembered that it belonged to his newly-acquired newspaper, a fact Bernard intended to ignore until they got home – if they got home.

They stayed at miserable, dingy hotels and had picnic meals of bread and cheese, with thimblefuls of wine. It was all utterly out of character so, knowing it couldn't last, Penny took action.

'I'm giving us all a surprise,' she announced brightly.

'She hasn't got her phrase book out has she?' said Simon

in panic.

'A *nice* surprise. I've discovered 500 francs I didn't know I had. I'm going to buy us all a slap-up dinner.'

'You should save the money,' grunted Bernard.

'It's my money. I found it at the bottom of my purse.'

'You ought to be more careful . . .' began Bernard, but his taste buds were already functioning.

'I shall have a sirloin steak,' said Penny, inexorably. 'Or, perhaps, steak au poivre. I shall start with avocado vinaigrette . . . I'm told,' she went on, 'there's an awfully good little place near Mont Claude. Remember, we called there on the way out? We're not far from it now. So, for our own self-respect, we'll stay somewhere a bit better than last night's crummy joint. *And*, it's all on me.'

Bernard sulked for a bit, then said, 'What's this place called?'

Next morning, Bernard was in a mood to linger. 'Did a lot of mileage yesterday. I'm a bit whacked. I'd like to go round that château again. May not be so many people there and I might get a chance of seeing those tapestries properly . . .'

He sauntered off alone. Halfway to the château, he realized he was very tired. The concentrated driving had taken its toll of his energy after the strain of the past few weeks. He entered a café and ordered a cognac. Instantly, he felt better, and ordered another. After three he didn't feel at all fatigued, so he ordered one more for good luck, and then walked briskly to the castle. A coach-load of British tourists and a few visitors from private cars were about to go in, and he trailed behind them. There weren't sufficient written guides in English to go round so the human guide said, in thick Parisian tones, that he would endeavour to speak to

172

the visitors in their own language, which he did, lapsing fairly frequently into French. No one understood a word but all listened obediently. After his introductory remarks he ushered the party down the long corridor to the first chamber. Bernard stayed behind to look at a tapestry he had not noticed on his previous visit. The guide called him, firmly but cordially. Bernard ignored the summons. The guide tugged at the sleeve of Bernard's anorak. 'Don't you touch me!' cried Bernard. They were now in the corridor and the crowd had seeped through into the big chamber where they were standing, bovinely, waiting to be told what to admire. On impulse Bernard hit the guide, who fell at his feet, more from fear of being hurt than from the actual blow. Bernard swiftly took the bunch of keys, locked the door from the hall behind them, clouted the guide again, for good measure, and walked into the crowded chamber, locking that door also.

'Ladies and Gentlemen,' he announced, 'our guide has had to attend to a party of his own countrymen, and he's asked me to take over. Now this is the Agnes Sorel room; that is a portrait of her over the chimney breast. It was painted by Eugène Delacroix, as, of course you all know.' They duly stared, in some surprise, at the portrait of a bearded warrior. One or two of them shifted uncomfortably, wondering if they were facing in the wrong direction.

'On the right,' continued Bernard, 'is a tapestry depicting the triumphal arrival of Napoleon at the gates of Moscow. Napoleon was one of Agnes' dream men, which was why she fell out with King François the first – known as François Première. He it was he who consigned her to the dungeons which we shall visit later.' Bernard heard a muffled shout from the corridor and pronounced that there was little else of interest in this room, so they should proceed to the next, into which they were duly locked.

'The king's bedroom,' he announced. 'Very convenient for

173

Agnes, you might think, but in fact he never slept in it. I know what *you're* thinking,' he said to a jolly woman in a pillar-box red hat and a two piece gleaming mauve nybroleen suit, 'and I daresay you're right.' She laughed appreciatively as did most of the others, including a portly man, with distinguished grey hair and sharp jaw, who remarked, 'I'm enjoying this. And I never had much thirst fristry.' Bernard detected another muffled sound from the rear so he quickly shepherded the crowd through two more doorways, which he locked and bolted.

'The ceiling in this splendid room,' he began, 'was painted by . . . so difficult to see by these 40-watt bulbs, isn't it? Ceiling was painted by . . . anyone like to guess? Not Watteau, eh?'

The jolly lady laughed. 'What-ho,' she repeated, liking the sound. 'He's a what-ho, all right.'

'And,' said Bernard, 'certainly not by Cézanne.'

'Says-anne,' chortled the lady in mauve. 'I'll give 'im says-anne.'

'Actually it's an Italian masterpiece by Leonardo's friend, Guiliamo Suffitto – William the Ceiling, as our Welsh friends would say – who popped over here, lay on his back for several months, and created what you now see.' They all stared upwards through the gloom at a murky area of fading cherubs against an orange-brown sky.

'The bod's first class,' said the grey-haired man.

'What-ho!' said the plump lady in mauve as Bernard invited her to mount the stone steps to the rampart walk. 'You're a card! Says-anne!' She gurgled happily and panted as she climbed the two hundred and forty-three steps.

Bernard decided it was time for a dignified retreat. He hurried the party round the ramparts and down into the hall where monarchs and aristocrats had once held councils and plotted murders. Here he gave a final peroration. 'I hope I have adorned for you a little this colourful episode in French history. Don't forget to look at the portrait of the Duc de Biriatou as you go out. A handsome man, standing there all dandified, with three quivering borzois at his heels. Wicked man, he locked his poor old grey-haired mother up in the dungeons at Loches, just because she didn't marinate the cherries properly one Sunday when she was supervising lunch.'

'Her-her!' chortled the mauve lady. 'That's rich. Marinate! Her-her!'

'Thank you, ladies and gentlemen, for your attention. This way out, please.' Bernard collected over 100 francs and, at the gate to the château, was stopped by the grey-haired man who said. 'Great stuff, young man. What you do for a living?'

'I'm a journalist. On a sabbatical, you know.'

'Well, there's a coincidence. We're in the same game. I own the *Daily Moon*. Name's Waterbeech. Lord Waterbeech. Always looking for a bit of culture to add to the *Moon* . . . in a pop way. Something entertaining, like what you did today. How about becoming our History Correspondent?'

Bernard walked briskly down the hill away from the château feeling elated. Outside the café where he had drunk the four cognacs sat two familiar figures.

'You got through that Italian trip a bit pronto then?' said Bob. 'You remember Idaho, who won the porn prize?'

Bernard did, and thought the writer looked more human in an open-necked shirt and jeans than in the electric blue suit he had worn to accept the award.

'Have to be on my way,' said Bernard. 'What brings you here?' His elation was ebbing away; assaulting a guide might well be an offence.

'On our way back to Draggynyong,' said Bob. 'We're in a restrong situation now, Bernie. That Monsieur Charles was a bit upset about Idaho using the Ombragée for his book so we bought him out. We just been to Paris to arrange the finance. Know what we're doing? We're opening a chain of porno restrongs all over France. And we got Rodge to design and paint all the doors for us. And the walls. Rodge is into walls now.'

'I'll look forward to writing them up for my new employer,' said Bernard. 'Cheers.'

'Hey! What about your old employer?' Bob exclaimed.

'What about him?'

'Haven't you heard?'

'Not a word. Car radio doesn't work over here.'

'We-ell,' said Bob. 'He's been excommunicated.'

'Proggle?'

'Sure.'

'For what?'

'He was goin' to present the Pope with some missal, right?'

'That's what we were all bumming around Italy about.'

'So. He promised this church in Frascati this huge amount of money.'

'I heard about that.'

'And he promised the Pope this holy book they had there, which the Pope was goin' to sell to the Aye-rabs?'

'Right,' said Bernie.

'And Proggle goes along to the Vatican to present this

book, doesn't he?'

'Did he?'

'Sure. And he gets it out of its little box and what happens?'

'It disintegrates,' said Bernard. 'Because it hasn't seen the light.'

'That's quick, son. And very good. But not what happened.'

'Go on.'

'Proggle presents it to the Pope and . . . what do you think this little old book is?'

'What?'

'A copy of the Koran.'

Bernard fell about telling Penny. 'It must have been Donald. He really is devious that uncle of mine. I wonder what happened to him?'

'Now it's my turn. I've been fooling around with this radio here since we got back from the swimming pool, and I got B.B.C.'

'So . . .'

'Uncle Donald has turned up in Moscow, if you please, with one of the original missals. Must be the Frascati one. He's sold it to the Russians for a huge sum of money . . .'

'Surely he doesn't want to stay in Russia?'

'He's already left.'

Bernard felt dazed.

'And he really is a very devious man, that uncle of yours, as you say. Because the copy the Russians have got and paid for is a photographed copy. Donald is returning the original to the church in Frascati where he left the copy of the Koran which Proggle got hold of . . .'

'In his wily wizened way!'

'And the Pope is making him a Count of the Holy Roman Empire for his services. So he really will have a title.'

'The old fraud. That won't go down well with Proggle.'

In the Plum family home at Osidge, North London, the scene was one of domestic bliss. Bernard was at the sink drying up the supper crocks, Penny, seated at the dining table, was attempting to reconcile her bank statement with the rather larger figure she had supposed to be standing to her credit, and the boys were putting finishing touches to a map of Western Europe, indicating the route they had followed during the previous summer.

'Think I'll watch *Measure of the Day*,' said Bernard. 'Then I can pull faces at Gideon.'

Gideon Apthorpe-Harebrook, after his sojourn in Fleet Street, was restored to former glory as a telecaster commentating on current affairs. His famous smirk was wider and more twisted than in the old I.T.A. days, and he had now taken to wearing spectacles with frames like two pears joined together where their stalks had been, and carefully constructed so as to highlight the upper contour of his smirk. Bernard was glad he tuned in because there, seated beside Gideon were Arthur, Lord Proggle, looking ill-at-ease, and Donald, positively oozing sang-froid. He was just in time to hear his uncle being introduced as

'Dr Donald Ardrake, the celebrated antiquarian.'

('Doctor!'

'Hush, Pen, this could be fun.'

'Not with Donald in it,' said Simon. 'I'd rather have scenery.' He turned his back ostentatiously, nevertheless lingering within sight of the flickering box.)

'There would seem,' said Gideon blandly, a lord of the atmosphere, for all that the colour of his hair on Bernard's set was bright green, 'to have been criticism in high places about this E.E.C. cheese mountain in which you've been involved, Lord Proggle. It's good of you to come along and talk to us. Would you say – as some have said – that you have made an unfairly large profit from it?'

'Wouldn't – ah – say anything of the sort.' Proggle leered at the camera and showed his lime-green teeth, which made Bernard twiddle a knob. 'Perfectly straightforward deal. Done a lot of – ah – people a lot of – ah – good.'

'Is that your view, Dr Ardrake?' Bernard's adjustment had turned his hair orange but Gideon, unaware of this, remained as smooth as ever. 'I understand you have been in the U.S.S.R. selling a rather different commodity . . .'

'It's *Count* Ardrake, actually, dear heart. His Holiness, you know . . .'

'Of course, dear Count, I do apologize. It has been whispered, Lord Proggle, that you had hoped for similar preferment from the Pope?'

'We – ah – here to talk about newspapers, or not? I thought this was about newspapers.' Proggle looked so furious that as Bernard twiddled knobs again the sweat dripping from his brow became tangerine.

'Would you say, Count, that the Italians are angry about this deal?'

'I should say absolutely certainly they are. Having to buy

179

back their own cheese, via the Arabs, in that wily wizened way, but they think, dear heart, that they've bought rather more than they intended to.'

'More cheese, do you mean, Count?'

'Not exactly . . .'

'Lord Proggle,' cooed Gideon, with studied gentility, a sure sign to regular viewers (who did not necessarily see him in the brown ochre of Bernard's screen) that he was about to make a frontal stabbing. 'I would like you to meet a very distinguished Italian journalist. Signore Leonardo Giovanni Dino-dino Caradente-Vecchio, from Rome. Are you there, Dino?'

The face of Dino, appeared, monitored, on another screen.

'Hallo, Mr Gideon, and good evening the Lord Proggle, Countless Ardrake.'

'You have been doing some research, I believe, Dino, into this cheese mountain – er – scandalo, as you call it.'

'Also, into the missing missal, Mr Gideon . . .'

It was Donald's turn to look displeased, now in scarlet.

'But that has been returned surely?' Gideon expressed shock, another sure sign of revelations to come.

('Now that it's become black and white do leave it alone, Bernie.')

'Here in Roma,' said Dino, 'it is being said that the missal presented to the Pope is a fake, and the one left in Moscow . . .'

'That's a black lie, dear heart. His Holiness confirmed its genuine quality . . .' Proggle, the pressure off himself and on Donald, relaxed for a moment.

'I say only it is being said, Count. Nothing is proved. But experts, antiquarians. I think they are very tricky peoples. Hard to convince . . .'

'I am not going to sit here, Mr Apthorpe-Harebrook . . .'

'Please stay, Count. Let's finish about the cheese mountain . . .'

'I am sorry, Mr Gideon. Yes, I would like to ask Lord Proggle about this.' Dino held up a round cheese, removed a section from the top, and pulled out a small plastic bag which appeared to have a rock cake inside. 'I think your viewers are a little misunderstood, yes? They do not know what I am doing. I tell you. This little package contains what you call "pot". Marijuana. Hidden inside the cheese.'

The cameras all panned on to Proggle who exclaimed, blinded by such an excess of light, 'But Darien said there was no possible way – ah – could be discovered.'

'Lord Proggle, would you like to say whom you mean by Darien?'

Proggle looked with hatred at Gideon and rose. 'No,' was all he could manage as he cursed himself for having made such a stupid remark. It was all the fault of having taken wine to allay his nervousness. It had been his downfall before. He stumbled out of range of the cameras, tripping over numerous thick flexes and causing alarm, not for his safety, but for the expensive equipment he might damage.

'Would it be Mr Darien Avonbury, Deputy?' shouted Dino, in triumph.

'I don't think I can allow that.' The smirk grew so pronounced that its upper limit disappeared behind Gideon's pear-shaped spectacle frames.

'Never mind. I like to talk to your other guest, Mr Gideon.'

'Please do.'

'I think, Count, you have a visitor there in London, very anxious to see you . . .'

As Bernard played again with the knobs Donald looked

181

alarmed in sky-blue. The cameras concentrated on the entrance to the set where the figure of M Vesoul, of La Vielle Ferme de Brieu, appeared. He waddled forward, double-chinned, double-paunched, everything a little accentuated with the passing of time. He shook hands with Gideon, with Donald, and then strode to the side of the set and shook hands with various technicians. Whilst this was going on Gideon (vermilion in Osidge) was telling the viewers about Vesoul. 'And it is his assertion, Count Ardrake, that you arranged another food mountain, to do with the apples he grows in his Normandy orchards?'

'Yes, well,' replied mauve-nosed Donald, 'all that's true. All arranged with Brussels, as Monsieur Vesoul knows. Everything thoroughly above board.'

'Is not so.' Vesoul rushed to the centre of the set, confronting Donald. 'You agree price with me in pounds, yes?'

'Pounds sterling we call them.'

'I call them pounds tricky, monsieur. I lose much money because pound falls against franc, yes?'

'I can't control the foreign exchange markets, dear heart.'

Vesoul narrowed his now primrose-yellow eyes. 'But not mind that, monsieur. What about the missal, yes? You promise me missal to present to my church. So that all tourists come to St Martin-sur-Cadeau. *That* what you tell me, I get for my apples, apart from pounds sterling. And you get my apples dirt cheap.'

'Dear heart, but of course.' Donald in close-up was, appropriately, in high purple. 'The missal I promised you is in my care. But you didn't expect I would entrust it to the post? I was going to bring it to you at your splendid farm. Have you any of that excellent Sancerre, still?'

'Excuse me, gentlemen,' said Gideon, 'but I was under the

impression, Count Ardrake, that you had presented the original missal to the Pope . . .'

'Right, dear heart.'

'And the copy of it, to the Russians?'

'Well, that was what was put about.'

'You mean you didn't present it to the Russians?'

('An international incident is coming up,' said Bernard, as the screen went blood red.)

'Not, not actually.'

'But you are going to present the copy to M Vesoul here?'

'Copy?' screamed M Vesoul, his violet lips dissolving rapidly into dark grey. 'It was not copy you promised when I sell my apples cheap. You tell me . . .'

'Surely,' said Donald grandly, 'you wouldn't wish me to palm off a copy on his Holiness . . .'

'But people not come to see a *copy* . . .'

'*I* will sign it for you.' Donald went into the purple again.

'Forgive me, Count Ardrake.' Gideon was so excited that he removed his pear-shaped spectacles, revealing russet-coloured eyes, 'but what was it that you presented to the Soviet authorities?'

'That was a little naughty, I grant you. But I think they deserve it. I gave them a fake manuscript. But written and illuminated in medieval Latin of course.'

'And it was a sacred work?'

'You could call it that.'

'What was it?'

'*1984*.'

Gideon asked if it was this illuminated Orwell manuscript for which the Russians had paid thousands of roubles.

'Dear heart, don't be disturbed. They cannot possibly object. I have given all the proceeds to Amnesty International.'

('Perhaps,' Penny suggested, as several hundreds of shocking-pink Gideons whooshed maniacally up the screen, 'we should start building our deep shelters now.'

'Alors,' said Simon.

'Prego,' said Brian.)